The Brain Harvest

AUTOBIOGRAPHICAL NARRATIVES
&
OTHER FICTIONS

Ken Nash

ISBN 978-0-9571213-1-7

Equus Press
Birkbeck College (William Rowe), 43 Gordon Square, London,
WC1 H0PD, United Kingdom

Typeset by lazarus.
Printed in the Czech Republic by PB Tisk

Composed in 10pt Sabon, designed by Jan Tschihold (1967), & Snell, designed by Matthew Carter, based on the roundhand of George Snell.

Baskets 5
Three Sisters 17
The Day I Met My Parents 21
The Two Lives of Edward Hopper 26
Mattress World 31
The Dibble & Emily Dickinson 37
The Cello Garden 41
Game Theory for Beginners 52
Maurice Utrillo 57
The Brain Harvest 59
Making Babies 65
The Last 69
My Lobotomy 73
Phaedra 77
The Habits 80
The Blue Bedouins 83
My Roommate's Girlfriend 87
Taking Care of Montreal 91
Lightning Strikes Again 94
Melissa's Creations 99
The Book Group 101
The Hostage 105
Anima Husbandry 110
What a War! 113
The Replacement 116
Missing 121
We Celebrities 125
The Patch 127
Shelly's Café 131
Event Horizon 138
The Reagan Years 145
The Great Simanoa 159

Baskets

I'm pretty used to telling this story now. Not a week goes by when someone doesn't see my sign on the side of the road, come wandering up the path and ask me about the baskets. They are always amazed by what I show them. When they ask about my company, I explain that it's just me, that I make them on my own. They often appear incredulous. So I tell them this story. It's about meeting Olaf Grünbaum, the old basket maker, and how it changed everything I thought about baskets – everything I thought about the world, really.

The year before I met Grünbaum, I had started working for Global Basket International (GBI) the world's largest, most powerful basket maker.

"You're lucky you're starting in Bark," said my coworker Michelle. "Most new hires start in Straw and Pine Needles."

I hadn't thought of it that way. I expected to start out warping and wefting my way as a weaver, not as a sorter. I had no idea of the scale and complexity of the basket industry.

Six years of university studies hardly prepared me for corporate basketry with its hierarchical command structure, government oversights, fluctuating domestic and global sourcing, logistics management and waste control.

I had graduated top five of my class. My master's thesis "The Three Problematic Odd-Grid Patterns of Celtic Frieze Knots" was published in the highly respected Weave Theory and Practice Quarterly. Professors gushed about my work on curvatures in six-fold symmetries.

But all that knowledge and education mattered very little at GBI, where I systematically separated bark shavings by quality, shade, texture and weight day after day. Yet how could I complain? I had beaten out dozens, if not hundreds, for my position. Many of my former classmates were doing time spinning flax or braiding rugs, if they were lucky to be working at all.

My supervisor, Mike Samuels, entered the room, calling out instructions, wireless communication headset clipped to his shaved and polished scalp and a GPSX Time Tracker in hand.

"Dawkins," he said. "Personnel needs you downstairs ASAP. Paperwork."

"I was just there this morning."

"That was for your security clearance and non-disclosure agreement. You still gotta do your I-49's, your Q-14's and your G-NAT's."

I had no idea what he was talking about.

"Good luck," said Michelle, "Those G-NAT's are a bitch."

I set aside the three lengths of Vancouver Flat Ash I was working with, brushed the splinters off my tie and headed downstairs to Personnel to complete yet another set of forms.

In all, during my first year at GBI, I probably spent as much time completing paperwork, attending staff meetings, conferences and motivational seminars as I did doing actual sorting. The sorting itself was mind numbing. Tedious. All those theories I learned –

evolution of aboriginal weaves, chromatic strip pattern arrays, the five genera of isonemal motifs – all that was so deeply ingrained in my memory was quickly becoming nothing more than vague recollections, overshadowed by my increasing skills in Excel spread-sheets, SQL Servers, matrix barcoders and PowerPoint presentations.

"You're doing a bang up job, Dawkins," Samuels told me during one of my quarterly performance assessments. "Extremely low sorting error. Top notch speeds. Good punctuality. Areas to improve on... I suppose those would be communication and en-thu-*see*-asm, don't you?"

"I suppose so," I replied.

"You're a good worker, Dawkins," he said, nodding his headset and checking the timer on his memory pad. "I have faith you'll make bonus next quarter. Perhaps a promotion to Coiling by the end of the year, eh?"

It was basically the same review I'd received every time – that elusive golden loom of bonus and advancement dangled before me. Once again.

It did not come as a great surprise for most of us when the layoffs came. The war in the Near East and Central Asia had dried up imports of some of our most utilized resources: Cambodian Vine Rattan, Sinai Braided Sea Grass, Singapore Cane, Burmese Celery Hemp, Uyghur Cave Moss... Nearly half the staff in various departments lost their jobs, including a number of managers like Samuels. Michelle, by that time, had advanced to Handle Binding and, with her father's connections to the company's CFO, her continued employment at GBI was virtually assured.

"This sucks," Michelle told me at lunch on my final day. "No advance notice. No severance. You'd think the world's largest basket maker could do better than that. Maybe you're better off getting out of this sinkhole. Someone with your skills and brains is bound to do okay no matter what."

"Thanks for saying that," I said, picking through my plate of Panda Express curry noodles. "But it's hard to say what will happen. Nobody's hiring. And the recruiters have a six month wait before they'll even talk to you."

Michelle stopped gnawing at her spring roll and looked thoughtfully for a moment. "Listen, Ted. I don't know if this would help you or –"

"Yes?"

"Well, I have an uncle, a great uncle, who does baskets."

"'Does baskets'? What does that mean? He designs them? Exports them? Markets them?"

"He makes them. All by himself. I know that sounds a bit crazy. But everyone says his work is really fantastic. I mean – I'm not sure what he can offer, but maybe he can help. Like show you how to go into business for yourself."

Business for myself? The idea spun around in my head and it felt good. Watch my own business grow and expand until maybe one day it could actually rival GBI for market dominance. Crush them. Reduce GBI to nothing more than a minor domestic player in the basket game. Isn't that how it works? The small and lean start-up eventually overtakes the self-satisfied Goliath? It was a crazy, quixotic idea. But it was worth at least meeting the old man and seeing his setup.

To call Grünbaum a renegade is not actually correct. The thought never crossed his mind to join or rebel against the corporate world. Orphaned at a young age, he was taken in by the Tsimshian Indian community where he was eventually initiated into the tribe and taught their customs and crafts. For them, basket weaving was a sacred act. The Great Goddess had spun the world into existence and each basket they produced was a recreation of that divine act.

Upon reaching manhood, Grünbaum set out to discover the world. In the Kashmir valley, beneath the Himalayas, he learned to dye and lace young willow twigs and monsoon grass into great matrimonial baskets. From the African Zulus he was taught to tightly weave the waxy ilala palm fronds into geometric patterns to create watertight vessels.

From the Inupiat in Alaska he learned to work with black plankton fibers removed from the mouths of baleen whales and how to carve walrus tusks into ornate handles. From the Cherokee in Oklahoma he learned the challenging double-weave rivercane technique and their sixty-seven different words for *basket*.

From the Japanese, he learned to design *hanakago*, bamboo flower baskets. In the Peruvian rainforest, he climbed Chambira trees to collect the spiky young palms they boiled, dyed and braided with beads. From the Greeks he learned the ancient skills of the Canephorea, weaving wool baskets for sacrificial ceremonies.

In Bavaria he learned the art of the Travel Basket, or *Reisen Korb*, a light basket made to carry small provisions – as well as Time itself. And, while harvesting the bark of black ash in the Adirondack, the Shaker community he lived amongst taught Grünbaum the importance of weaving work together with prayer.

With each culture he learned new materials, techniques and designs, as well as the stories, myths and legends that went with them.

Eventually, he assimilated all these techniques and ideas into his own method of working, perfecting a type of seven-fold symmetry, which is highly unique. (All this he told me upon our first meeting, while sipping tea brewed from fresh mint and ginger he'd collected in the forest around the old renovated and modernized hunting lodge that was his home and workshop.) I could hardly believe what he was telling me. Apparently he managed to accomplish all these years of extensive R&D without investors, endowments, fellowships or grants.

I came prepared with a list of questions, such as *What is your production rate? What channels of distribution do you use? What percentage of gross sales do you take?*

Grünbaum smiled and laughed away my questions. "My boy, my boy… You need to forget *all* your old ideas about baskets, all they taught you in school and in business. They taught you how to weave empty baskets. I will teach you how to weave baskets that are full – full of life, full of spirit. With such baskets you will never want for anything."

"Okay, sure. But who does your marketing? Do you have a website?"

"Listen to me," said old Grünbaum, resting a hand upon my shoulder. "I know it may come as a surprise to you, but during my life I have never sold one single basket."

What was this? Never sold a basket? And I traveled six and a half hours to bumfuck nowhere to find this crazy old bastard thinking he could offer me some sort of concrete advice. Never sold a basket? Never made a single dollar from his work? How did he survive?

Grünbaum smiled and nodded as if reading my thoughts. "I know this is difficult for you to comprehend and I don't expect you to understand just now. It took me nearly twenty years to learn the secret, but I am ready to pass on my knowledge if you're willing to be patient and learn."

"I'm listening," I said, though thinking it may not be too late in the season to get temporary employment as a bark shaver on a birch farm.

"Look around you," said Grünbaum. "Everything here was provided for me by the spirits in return for creating soulful works of beauty."

Grünbaum explained that by simply creating his baskets, all that he needed to live appeared for him, as if brought during the night by magic elves. Right. Sure. That was it for me. I was ready to leave.

But then – at the far end of the room – what was this? A basket, surely. But like none I'd ever seen.

Grünbaum acknowledged my gaze. "Come, I will show you." He rose unsteadily from his chair. "It's nearly complete."

I could a scarcely imagine anything more complete. It was as if seven young willow boughs became enraptured by a Bach sonata, entwining themselves amidst air, light and variegated organic matter, in apparently seamless precision. The basket was dyed with the blood of cranberries, myrtle and black walnut, then threaded with gold hairs of straw and hemp. Pale asphodels and a dark mottling of pond grass danced sprightly in and out of its lyrical wicker staff.

"Stay," he said. He took his seat before the worktable and began threading more asphodels between nearly invisible gaps in the warp of the basket. "I will show you everything."

And he did. Or as much as he could during those nine months before death's irreversible uncoiling of life from bone.

Grünbaum worked tirelessly from sunrise until sunset, gathering materials from the forest floor and high up in the trees; peeling, drying and pounding out bark and plant fibers; boiling the blooms, berries and nuts for dyes; tapping tree sap; distilling plants, bark and insects into resin; sanding, glazing and varnishing materials; and slowly, patiently weaving the great lot of resources into amazing baskets.

He worked with calm, focused intensity, showing amazing attention to every aspect of design. Even a basket interior – something no one in the industry gave much thought to – was painstakingly detailed.

"In the fourth dimension," Grünbaum enigmatically explained, "the exterior and interior are simultaneously visible."

His interior weaves were often comprised of spiraling patterns of heather and mayweed, finished off with a soft luster of wax from local beehives or carnauba palms.

Heather was perhaps his favorite foliage – this for its range of violaceous colors, as well as its pliability and unique taste. He worked it like a painter applying oils. He ran its sinuous stems through his long, grey whiskers, wetting them with his lips, before threading them in and out of the white willow framework.

It's no wonder a single two-handled carrying basket could take up to eight weeks to complete. Sometimes longer.

When nearly finished, Grünbaum would spring to his feet, telling me to get ready. This was the moment. This was what it all led up to. A sort of christening ceremony. A ritual. I don't remember what he called it. But for Grünbaum it was the most crucial part of the whole creative process.

By evening we were prepared for the ceremony. We'd hurry outdoors no matter what the weather. The radiant coastal sun would set amidst a great unraveling of light. Pink and gold threads of luminosity slowly licked their way through the expanding shadows of fern, grass, lichen and leaves.

As the sun reeled in its gossamer strands, Grünbaum and I would hurriedly amass a large pyre of fallen timber, forest detritus and unused work materials. Once lit, this mighty bonfire would shoot blue sparks and white flames high into the night sky. The light cast forth set loose the silhouettes of plants and trees. Shadows danced ecstatically amongst the cedars to the choral pop, hiss and snap of the fire's conflagration.

While the fire was fully ablaze, old man Grünbaum would bend to his knees, bow his head and chant a prayer, thanking the spirits for all they provided. Then – I almost fell over with astonishment the first time I saw it – he would take the basket, the fruit of his long weeks of labor, and toss it high into the night sky. The basket would ascend, spinning into a sphere, then stop amidst the stars for a moment before plummeting back toward the fire. Flames reached up like arms drawing the basket into their yearning embers. At such moments, I could feel the breath sucked out of me, as if I too were being drawn into that ravenous pyre.

I'd watch in amazement as the fire quickly devoured the delicate flesh of the basket. Soon nothing remained but a cage of charred ribs, which then collapsed upon itself. The oddest sensation would come over me. Grünbaum called it a feeling of weightlessness.

"Permanence and continuity are not as you imagine them," he told me. "When you see beyond appearance you can experience the indeterminate ideal."

That was typical of Grünbaum's way of speaking. Don't ask me to explain. I am a basket maker, not a philosopher. A craftsman, not a metaphysician. If Grünbaum's work somehow transcended craft, or even art for that matter, it did so not in the fulfillment of an ideal basket, but in heeding some metaphysical itch he needed to scratch.

Still, however, his words stay with me, even after all these years.

Michelle, in a black wool dress, cedar buttons from the neck down to her knees, stood atop the granite cliff, one hand continually pulling wind-blown hair away from her eyes, the other holding out the white lacquered urn. She turned it over. Dark ash trailed out like a swarm of flies and ascended over the ocean.

Mourners were few. There was Michelle, her family and various cousins. There was also an older stepbrother from the Tsimshian tribe, who came wearing traditional Tsimshian mourning attire of goat wool and spruce roots, and jewelry of beaver claws and clam shells.

Quietly, beneath the shade, stood an elderly couple that lived down the trail from Grünbaum. Their daughter, Lee, visiting from Seattle, was with them. Hovering around, taking photographs, was Jamison Crowell, a journalist from the local Observer newspaper and great admirer of Grünbaum.

To my surprise, no one asked, Where are the baskets? They simply took it as a matter of course that the baskets would be gone, sold, given away or whatever he did with them.

But they did talk baskets. At great length. Every person could, and did, recount the various baskets they saw taking shape over the years. They spoke in detail. And their words perhaps more vividly brought the baskets to mind than if the actual baskets had been placed before us.

Grünbaum's brother burned incense and shook a snakeskin rattle. He chanted a prayer in Tsimshian and said to me, "Friend, do you have any weed?"

Today, in my seaside workhouse, my fingers work to a rhythm that seems to come from the evolving hollow of the basket. Weaving has become intuitive and baskets form from my hands as easily as breath flows from my lips. I work tirelessly, my few interruptions being mainly for food, sleep and the occasional visitor who comes to inquire about baskets.

With Michelle's help, I found this place. Its large windows overlook a forest of eucalyptus trees and flowering heather. To her father's dismay, Michelle left GBI to be here with me. She soon began weaving her own baskets. Quite exquisite. Using vines allayed with a balm of petals and leaves. In her spare time she is researching a book on basketry in ancient and sacred texts.

Together, however, we've begun something new. A collaboration of sorts. I watch in amazement each day as this new creation expands beneath her skin. With the tips of my fingers, I can feel the wondrous coils of life wreathing together. We have decided to name her Penny, after Michelle's great-grandmother Penelope.

I consider myself fortunate to be one of the few to witness old Grünbaum's work. And I'm very grateful for all he taught me – though I can't say I was ever really convinced by all that talk about the spirits providing for him. I sometimes wonder if there had been a stealthy accomplice, secret admirer or clandestine acolyte who stocked the cupboards and closets while we were out gathering materials or asleep at night.

I don't know.

But it doesn't really matter. Even though I've never managed to bring myself to burn one of my own baskets, I still live as though the spirits provide for me. And in a way they do. Because every time I tell this story – more and more, lately – I sell another basket.

Three Sisters

When I was very young – and, oh, this was a long time ago, back during the Depression when everyone was just doing what they could to get by and had no big plans for the future – when I was, I guess, around twelve years old, I spent a lot of time with chickens, teaching them to do things, baiting them with seed, prodding them with sticks and chasing them around the yard, yelling at them, trying to get them to remember their commands.

Don't let anyone tell you different, chickens are dumber than dumb. But if you are patient and persistent enough you can get them to do things. They don't understand what they're doing, but they'll do it – just like a piece of clay doesn't understand you're making a sculpture, but with enough kneading and pulling it will become that thing you're trying to create. And that's exactly how I set about getting the chickens to perform Chekhov's *Three Sisters*.

I found a copy of *Three Sisters* on a shelf in the basement where Mom's old things were kept. I think maybe she performed in it years ago in New York, long before I appeared in her life. I didn't question whether it was an appropriate choice or not for chickens. Probably not. But once I began reading and thinking about how to get chickens to portray the various roles, I became inspired by this play and the theatrical possibilities it offered.

True, it is difficult for chickens to convey emotion. And even more difficult to get them to speak ponderous lines such as, "Happiness is not for us, nor will it be. We can only wish for it." So basically I settled for having the chickens do a sort of improvisation around Chekhov's text, gesticulating, focusing their attention on one, then the other, crying out in despair, chirping happily, cackling orders or dispensing salutations with a fluttering of feathers. Getting them to drink tea and brandy was not so difficult, but long pauses were a fairly arduous task. And getting chickens to stand steady and appear lost in contemplation – that was my primary directorial challenge.

With the help of my brother John, I built a stage adjacent to the work shed. My sister Louise sewed black curtains pieced together from old oil rags, like the ones Dad used for auto repairs before he sold off the Packard. Proscenium footlights were made with candles set within old Maxwell House coffee cans. And the green room was, of course, made from green painted chicken wire. John, in his enthusiasm, wanted to dig an orchestra pit, but I felt the old chickens-pecking-at-piano-keys bit threatened to turn the whole production into a novelty act.

Opening Night. There were eight people in the audience. Six of them were family. But there was also Mr. Sayles, the postman and Bridgette Gunther, the retarded girl from next door. Reviews of that first performance were a bit mixed.

"I didn't understand *any* of it," said Clark, my eldest brother.

My father said, "Why, Theo, I've never seen anything quite like it."

Mr. Sayles said that they were some of the best

behaved chickens he ever did see.

"What about the play, though?" I prodded. "What did you think about the doctor? Could you tell what he was getting at when he placed his beak beneath his wing trying to convey that existence may only be an illusion?"

Mr. Sayles scrunched his brow and replied, "Doctor? One of them birds was a doctor?"

The next day we ironed out some of the kinks in the performance. I believe the chickens did a much better job with the pacing and blocking during that evening's show, particularly the more tempestuous third and fourth acts.

By the third performance, word had spread around town. We had about fifteen people over to see the show. Among the audience members was Eva Schaumberg, the new girl. She moved to our town from Boston to live with her great aunt. Some said she came from money. That's about all we knew. She didn't dress like the rest of us. That was for sure. Her dresses displayed ten times as many buttons and clasps as other girls' dresses; their fabrics captured and held light like the surface of Hinkley Pond at night. Louise said each of Eva's dresses probably cost more than our father made in an entire year with his new insurance job.

The fourth performance was a marked improvement on the rest. There were moments when the chickens seemed so absorbed in their parts you nearly forgot they were chickens. Particularly Masha who, during her mental breakdown in Act Four, was so thoroughly convincing the audience was stunned into total silence. Mrs. Flaherty, the butcher's wife, sat with eyes bulging open, gripping her purse as if trying to strangle it. And Eva Schaumberg – beautiful Eva, poised upon her milk crate – I could see a moist glistening of tears on her cheeks as she watched the drama unfold.

"A green oak grows by the curving shore,' intoned Masha with ruffled feathers and nervous chirps as she circled center stage. Her movements seemed to so perfectly convey Chekhov's words, I felt I was almost hearing them spoken out loud.

"A gilded chain on the oak tree hangs… a green cat… a green oak tree… I am all confused. A life gone wrong…"

Around and around Masha clucked and circled the stage.

Suddenly I had a flash of insight and it was as if I was suspended over the town looking down at all these people who live and work here. And they were all at the same time *individuals* and *a whole*, extending infinitely through the vertical space of self and infinitely through the horizontal space of place and society. And I felt like this old Russian guy Chekhov, whoever he was, must have been sitting in this same exact spot, watching it all extending infinitely in every direction, his heart full and heavy, his ink quill dipping and scattering each word, words like tiny seeds upon paper, strewing them out. Tossing them upon the stage. For us. For you and me. For all our needy hearts to follow.

The Day I Met My Parents

The day I met my parents, it was sunny and the grass was still glossy with the night's condensation, and the few clouds above, marring the slate blue sky, seemed reluctant to be there. Their names are Bernard and Elaine. I saw their ad in the back of a Sunday magazine supplement.

Eligible Parents
Bernard and Elaine Sommers
Immediate Availability
Phone: 508-574-9168.

It's funny. I hadn't even thought about having parents until I saw that ad. I saw it and thought, Why not? Why should I go through the rest of my life on my own, puzzling out my future, ungrounded, unmoored by the structural hold and gravitational pull of filial obligations? Sure, I could marry, but that's not the same thing. A wife is no substitute for parents. I mean, a wife could always leave you for another guy. But parents – they're pretty much stuck with you.

I walked with Bernard and Elaine through a park near my place and we talked about what it would mean if they became my parents. Or, rather, they told me. They wanted to make sure I knew exactly what I was getting into.

"Some people just don't understand the commitment of having parents," Bernard said. "Parents are always there. Even if you leave home and travel to a distant land, parents will always be there with you. Not literally, but inside your head."

"That's right," said Elaine. "We're a little like having mice in the attic. We squeak around up there." She pointed to her temple, squinted her narrowly plucked brows and smiled, revealing an entirely perfect set of white teeth.

"I had parents myself when I was about your age," Bernard said, "Grace and Henry. They were wonderful parents. But, you know, it doesn't matter how wonderful or problematic your parents are. Having parents is sort of a rite of passage. It's something people should just do. You'll always feel like something's missing in your life if you've never had parents."

We were strolling along the walkway beside the park's picturesque drainage pond. I was carefully avoiding the large Canadian goose turds, but Elaine's white patent leather pumps seemed oblivious to them.

"How I envy you," she said, "just setting out down life's winding path. Such new and precious moments. So much for you to see and experience."

"I suppose both of you have had quite interesting lives," I said.

"I was a pilot during the Korean war," said Bernard. "Killed a whole lot of them slimy little yellow-skinned reds. After that I decided to come back to the States, settle down and devote myself to parenting. Elaine here – I met her at a cousin's wedding. She was engaged to another fellow at the time – Todd Manning, a really nice guy who worked in sales for R. J. Nabisco – but when Elaine and I saw each other, sparks flew. There was no mistaking it. We knew we were each other's destiny."

Elaine blushed and said, "Some of it was the champagne. But I wasn't complaining when Bernard reached beneath the table and squeezed my inner thigh."

We heard heavy stomping and panting advancing on us from behind. The three of us stepped off the concrete onto the grass to let a group of slow, overweight joggers pass. The heavy dew immediately penetrated the canvas of my tennis shoes and soaked through my socks. The cuffs of Bernard's pin-striped pants darkened along the edges. He stepped back onto the sidewalk and began running in place, pumping his arms in an exaggerated motion, mocking the joggers as they moved away. Elaine reached for his arm and pulled it down.

"Bernard was quite an athlete at one time, as you can probably tell. Even at his age he's still in pretty good shape." She tenderly squeezed his forearm.

"What do you mean pretty good? I'm in tip top shape." Then, to me, he said, "I bet I could even outrun a young man like you."

"Maybe," I said.

"How much do you want to bet I can beat you from here to that bridge?"

"That's okay. I'm not interested in racing."

"Oh, come on now. Are you afraid of being beaten by an old man?"

"No, that's not it," I said. Trying to come up with an excuse I pointed to my wet shoes and said they were too soaked for running.

Bernard bent over and pulled off his black wing tips and socks. "Come on then, we'll race barefoot –

like I used to when I was a kid."

"Oh good, a contest," said Elaine, clapping her palms together.

"Look, I'd just rather not. I'm sure you're a fast runner." I looked at my watch. "And – oh – hey, would you look at the time? I gotta get back to my office and finish some stuff. Some proposals I'm working on. They need to be in the mail by the end of the day. Should have been mailed yesterday, actually."

Elaine's perfect teeth disappeared into her pale face. "What about your parents? Are you just going to forget all about us?"

"No, it's not that. It's just that –"

"No. No. We understand." Bernard put a consoling arm around Elaine. "You're a busy young man. You don't have time for parents. It's understandable, really. Elaine and I may not be the most perfect parents, but we try." He removed a white hanky from inside his jacket pocket and handed it to Elaine to blot her moistening eyes before the mascara began to run.

"Please. You both seem like you really, really care about being parents and I'm sure you make wonderful parents. I'm just not so sure I'm the type of guy to have parents. Or maybe I'm just not ready for them yet."

"Ah-huh," said Bernard as if I'd stated something very foolish and naïve.

"What?"

"Nothing. You run along and take care of business. Elaine and I – we'll manage just fine on our own."

"No, please. Sorry. I'm sorry," I said. And never stopped saying. And still say it. And will forever say it, whether I call them Mom and Dad or Bernard and Elaine, whether I am seated at their home, eating one of Elaine's defiantly inedible three-bean casseroles or whether I am a thousand miles away living in a hotel room while working on some foreign development project. Wherever I am, Bernard and Elaine are with me and I don't think I will ever, ever escape them.

The Two Lives of Edward Hopper

Summer, 1953. Edward Hopper was unable to paint for months. What was left to paint? Nothing. He pursued realism to its very end. The course ran off into emptiness, like the road to Coast Guard Beach, bitten off at the end by the hurricane of '38. Trying to proceed was hopeless. He risked plummeting into an abyss where not even the guiding beacons of Nauset Lighthouse could reach.

It was the year communists invaded America. They were everywhere. They filled the headlines of the Boston Globe, the New York Times, the Brewster Herald. Their names were whispered amidst the static of AM airwaves. In New England, the communists floated zeppelins, carefully constructed from cumulonimbus clouds, sea salt and gull feathers. They ran stealth recognizance missions up and down the coastline.

Hopper kept up with the news. Stalin died in March. Three months later he was reborn as a hydrogen bomb. In six days time, the Rosenbergs would pay the price for their atomic midwifery. The red menace was said to have infiltrated the postal service, the film industry, food service personnel – even street walkers were said to subsidize their income by passing along reports and photographs to Soviet agents disguised as gas station attendants, pharmacists, hot dog vendors, train conductors, soda jerks and Catholic priests. Hopper knew even the local whippoorwills were suspect, their whistles now sounding more strident and anthemic than like mere avian mating cries.

Hopper's roof was leaking. The brand new fucking roof of their Eastham cottage. He carefully positioned an old paint bucket on the wood floor. Every half hour he rushed over to empty and replace the bucket.

Hopper sat in an Adirondack chair by the open door, watching the tall grass undulate in the wind like green and silver waves. He thought of moving his easel here and trying to capture the effect. Then he decided he would rather eat week old clam chowder than paint another goddamn Cape Cod landscape.

Hopper longed to be in New York. When he was in New York, he longed to be in Cape Cod. When he was in Cape Cod, he longed to be in New York. "What sort of realist are you?" he asked himself. "A person who perpetually longs for what *isn't* is not a *real* realist."

During lunch, he caught a momentary flash of inspiration. "I will paint this Campbell's soup can! Just that. The can. Nothing else." By the time he squeezed out a full tube of crimson red, he realized it was a pretty stupid idea.

Nothing felt new to him anymore. Everything had been done. Not even Jo excited him in the way she once did. She had grown broad in the hips. The sour skin of her buttocks had begun to curdle. He grew so accustomed to tuning out the screechy sound of her voice, she had started pummeling him with cutlery and houseplants just to get his attention before telling him anything important.

Technically, Hopper knew he was never going to be a better painter. He was too old to improve. There were now only three things he could do if he wanted to assure his place in art history. Stab Jackson Pollock repeatedly with a fork. Shoot himself in the head. Or single handedly capture a communist spy. He immediately ruled out capturing a communist spy. He wasn't entirely sure there even was such a thing as communism. Communism was like light; it had no true source, only its effects really existed.

Hopper stood in the doorway and watched the dark clouds moving overhead. There was a change in the air. The stench of sea awoke in his nostrils. After a moment, he realized something unusual was taking place in the sky. One of the clouds was moving much faster than the rest, nosing its way through the sulfurous haze.

Hopper stepped out into the rain. His balding, flattop head repelled the heavy drops. Streams of silver and white ran down the crevices of his face. He watched the cloud move through the sky toward his home. As it neared, he thought he saw lights blinking inside, like a bellyful of stars. The wind grew more intense. The tall grass whirled like ecstatic Sufi dancers. Jo's hydrangeas leaned forward and bowed their purple and blue heads. The grove of locust trees protectively wrapped their branches around each other.

Hopper wiped rain from his face, while still eyeing the cloud directly overhead. It slowed to a complete stop. Other clouds passed by. It struck him then; he had lived this moment before. This very moment. *Déjà vu*. Though it was not really this moment. It had been a moment like this, but from another lifetime.

Part 2

Hopper's previous life ended in the summer of 1953. That summer, Julius and Ethel Rosenberg, after making a daring prison escape, fled to Cuba to help Fidel Castro gain Soviet support for his revolution; Senator Joe McCarthy led a Senate inquiry regarding the possible abduction of American citizens by Russian spacecrafts; Albert Einstein had irrefutably proven the possibility of time travel; and Edward Hopper was placing the finishing touches on his painting *Sexy Robot Slaying Dragon in Outer Space*. His wife, Jo, had gone out to visit a friend, pick up mail, then buy groceries and a fresh bottle of scotch. That evening, they would celebrate the completion of his painting with a dinner of baked potatoes and fried cod, then play cribbage, get drunk, fight about money troubles, and fall asleep after making fetishistic love on the sofa.

Hopper knew he was at the height of his power as a painter. Yet he was lucky to sell just one or two canvases a year. His "sexy robot" paintings were not doing well. But they, at least, sold better than the *Jungle Vixens of Venus* series and the *Vampire Harlots Battling Squids* series before that.

His last dealer, Vivian Lieberman, suggested if Hopper ever wanted to become famous, he had only three options available to him: stab Jackson Pollock repeatedly with a fork, shoot himself in the head, or move to Italy were they were more likely to understand his visionary work than in America. Jo, in what Hopper described as "her usual narrow-minded and piggish way," refused to move to Italy.

The ceiling was leaking. The wind was picking up. Hopper was daydreaming about Tuscan villas and buxom, Mediterranean beauties with bare, grape-stained feet hefting wicker-wrapped jugs of Chianti upon their sienna tan shoulders.

Hopper stood in the doorway. The tall grass was bent by the wind into waves of silver and green. Scarlet dragon blood clung to the tip of his sable brush. He wondered if he had chosen the right path in life? What if he had stayed in Nyack and taken over his father's dry goods store? What if he had married young, started a family? Why is it we have only one life to experience? The impulse seized him to smash the sexy robot painting and denounce all art as a silly, useless contrivance. And the impulse to create, nothing but an absurd mental defect.

Hopper heard a loud mechanical screech. He turned toward the ocean. Dark clouds rolled towards the shore. One cloud, however, appeared almost luminous. It moved rapidly through the sky, passing other clouds along the way. As it neared Hopper's home, it turned slightly and slowed to a complete stop. The cloud was nearly translucent. It appeared to Hopper there were lead white specks, like stars, within it.

Something tumbled down from the cloud. It stopped several feet from the ground, nearly within Hopper's grasp. It was a rope ladder. It dangled there like an invitation. Such an event was like nothing he had ever dreamed up, yet it was real and happening at that very moment. Maybe at another time, another place, or in another life, he would have turned and run. But at this moment, he seized the opportunity, pulled himself up and began to ascend.

As Hopper rose toward the cloud, he wondered if perhaps the world was full of more possibilities than he had yet imagined. If even a simple cloud could contain such mystery, why not a lighthouse, a barn silo, an automat, a train compartment, a gas pump, an all night diner or a shaft of light in an empty room?

Mattress World

Irene Blueth was not prepared for the complexity of this endeavor. The salesman was clouding her thoughts. Posturpedic. Tempur-Pedic. Ultra Plus. Pillowtop. Pocket coil. Microtek foundation. Microporoscopic memory cells. He filled the air with words like a magician releasing doves from an empty cage.

"I know my mattresses inside and out," said Dwayne Campbell, his lips prying themselves apart to reveal a cumbrous smile. "What I don't know is your comfort level. Let's take a few moments today to figure that out, okay?" He nodded his head vigorously, waiting for signs of agreement.

A mattress was the key, Irene realized. On a late night TV advertisement, she had watched seven animated black arrows rise up through a fortress of coils and enter a woman's spine. The image immediately brought to mind something she'd seen earlier that day at the Main Library. The book *Chinese Plum-Blossom Needle Therapy* diagrammed the body's seven key points of receptivity. Tiny black arrows indicated their position along the spine and base of the skull. This was no coincidence, Irene thought. Someone or some *thing* was trying to tell her something.

That was how the trouble began. Someone *was*

trying to tell her something. She heard the voices while lying awake at night. They spoke over and over about water faucets, al-Qaeda, Hillary Clinton and Drew Barrymore. What any of it meant was unclear. The voices were garbled, sentences truncated. But she sensed their urgency. Millions of lives were at stake and it was up to Irene to do something. She could not understand *what* though. Sleeping in a heap of blankets on her cousin's old camping mattress was undoubtedly wreaking havoc upon her body's seven key points of receptivity. Only a new mattress would allow the voices to properly reach within her and clearly divulge their revelations.

To Dwayne Campbell, Irene Blueth seemed overwhelmed by her mattress options. "This is to be expected," his customer service trainer had forewarned him. "See the showroom from your customer's point of view. There are a plethora of choices. It's up to you to make the process easy."

Dwayne led Irene down the center isle to a white mattress with beige pinstripes. "The Queen Ann," he said, extending his arms to reveal the mattress's true magnificence. "A firm, extra-support mattress with a 27-per-square-foot coil count and plush granite support top. Give it a go."

Irene bent at the waist, pushed one hand into the mattress until it gave an inch, then stood straight again. This wasn't what she had in mind.

"Go ahead," encouraged Dwayne with his best customer service smile. "Feel free to lie down and get the full effect."

His sales training stressed how important it was to get the customer down on the mattress. *From a submissive posture, your sales message will more readily enter and guide their thoughts and choices.*

"Perhaps I can take your coat," he added. "That

might make this a little easier."

"I'm fine," said Irene Blueth. "Can I see the next one?"

Dwayne strained his facial muscles to keep the smile in place. This was not starting off quite right. Had he forgotten some vital step in his sales technique? He tried to quickly recall his SKESS, the Seven Key Effective Sales Steps he learned during his intensive three-day Mattress World Service Seminar. The only thing that came to mind, though, were the words his girlfriend Victoria used that morning.

"Lose this job, Dwayne, and that's it. You can move out and go live with your parents."

"My parents live in a retirement home in Vancouver," he reminded her.

"Then you'll have to find some other girlfriend who's willing to keep you afloat. It's not going to be me anymore. I've done all I can do, Dwayne."

She pulled her arms through her lavender jacket and flipped her long papaya conditioned hair out from beneath the collar. Then she turned toward Dwayne, appealingly. Her lovely mascara drenched eyes marked him with a look of pity.

"Poor Dwayne," she said, stepping closer. She kissed him on his receding hairline. "I love you, but I've had about enough." She brushed past him, took the keys to her Bimmer off the door hook and left.

Victoria, with her own condo, car and career plan, was the fireman's safety net that broke Dwayne's financial free fall after a quick succession of lost dot-com jobs and an uninsured emergency appendectomy. When he moved in with Victoria, it was the first place he'd ever lived with a bathtub, garbage disposal and liquid soap dispenser. Not to mention the canopy bed and NordicTrack exercise machine. He didn't know where he'd be without Victoria. Some transient hotel.

Standing in soup kitchen lines. Worse, maybe.

To Irene Blueth, the Brookner Ultra Plush looked like a pale blue pond with white petals floating atop the surface. A person could drown in a mattress like that, she thought to herself.

"Pardon me?" said Dwayne Campbell.

She felt a sudden intense craving for nicotine. "I'll be right back," she said, already on her way toward the door.

Dwayne stood helplessly by as his customer escaped the showroom. Fuck, he said to himself. Fuck. Fuck. Fuckety. Fuck. Fuck.

He walked back to the storeroom to check his hairline in the mirror and to roll more sports scented deodorant beneath his arms. When he returned a few moments later, he was relieved to see Irene Blueth pacing outside the front doors of the Mattress World showroom. The sale was not lost. He kept an eye on her while adjusting some hangtags and merchandise displays. He noticed her fervently smoking and immediately felt a stab of intense longing.

Smoking was, of course, off the menu for Dwayne, along with alcohol and drugs. He'd been clean for sixteen months and fourteen days – an accomplishment he viewed with a mixture of pride and lament. His old vices were the cause of great hardship for him, but they were also both loving and faithful. Now the only real pleasure left was sex, and Victoria began to frugally dole that out as if it were a sales incentive.

Irene Blueth trembled with anger. It was clear this sales agent was using diversionary tactics, trying to prevent her from purchasing a proper mattress. Instead he was showing her these complicated, overstuffed pincushions, which would only further muddle the voices trying to communicate to her.

Irene was losing patience. "Take deep breaths," she told herself. "Count to twenty. 1… 2…" A teenage girl on roller blades sped past, her wheels sounding like knives ripping through corrugated cardboard. "Watch it, you little bitch! 7… 8… 9…" An EMS vehicle blasted its horn as it rounded the corner onto Van Ness. "Goddamnit… 15… 16… 17…"

She needed to keep calm. She could not be confrontational with this sales agent. That approach had backfired at Bedroom Emporium. Also at Macy's Home Store, where the agents pretended they had no special acoustically perfect box springs. Ha! Did they take her for a fool? Unfortunately for the Free World, Macy's security guards prevented Irene Blueth from gaining the upper hand and bullied her out the back service doors.

Now she had a chance to try again. Dwayne Campbell – if that was indeed his real name – would unwittingly assist in her quest. He was weak. She could see that in the way his mollusk-like torso curled up beneath his powder blue power suit.

Dwayne Campbell smiled. He opened his arms welcoming Irene Blueth as she re-entered the showroom. He visualized "The Yes" just as he'd learned to do. Step Six: The Yes. *Thank you, Mr. Campbell for solving my sleeping needs!* Step Seven: Buyer Reassurance. *I'm just here to facilitate. It's the Ultra-Plush Micro-Stitch Dreamquest that you should thank!*

Irene Blueth would impose her will upon him, force him to take her behind the showroom to the vault where the special mattresses were kept. There she could lie down. Maybe all she needed was ten minutes. Ten minutes of perfect rest. Her body's seven key vital receptors would then have enough time to properly align themselves, clearly receive their instructions and allow Irene to fulfill her mission, saving perhaps millions of lives. Dwayne Campbcll would help her accomplish this. He must. It was as much his fate as her own.

The Dibble & Emily Dickinson

While my grandfather was writing his extensive biography on Emily Dickinson, he kept her dibble on his desk. It was the same cast-iron garden dibble Emily Dickinson used to inscribe the fertile soil surrounding her family's home in Amherst – the same one she clutched in her delicate bony palms and held to her heaving bosom each late spring as she gazed with wonderment upon the unfading world she had tenderly raised from seed.

Yet this very dibble was the cause of much bitterness and controversy in my grandfather's professional career. Many believed it should have been kept in a museum, locked within a glass case, not sitting atop the chaos of manuscript pages, index cards and deli wrappers of some little known scholar's cluttered desk. But my grandfather claimed he needed the dibble for his muse, that the dibble actually communicated with him, like a totem, like a holy relic. It told him things about Emily Dickinson that no one else ever knew.

For example, few people realized that at the age of twenty-nine, before the onset of agoraphobia, Emily Dickinson had a life-changing experience while out walking through the forest near Amherst. Strolling contemplatively amongst the paper birch, evergreens and parnassus, she happened upon what, at first, she believed was a massive, well-polished boulder. From this boulder emerged three small men in shiny green and yellow suits. They had large, almond shaped eyes and their scalps were as smoothly polished as the seemingly uninhabitable rock from which they emerged.

Thinking they were perhaps angels – possibly sent to convey a message from Heaven – she allowed them to lead her inside the elliptical stone structure. To her great surprise, it turned out to be a miraculous flying machine.

What happened inside, my grandfather wrote, was uncertain, but it was his belief she became part of one of the very first human cloning experiments.

Unquestionably, my grandfather's findings ruffled some feathers among academic circles. Many believed that the visions imparted to him from Emily Dickinson's dibble were not substantial enough proof of real events; they needed to be corroborated by empirical facts and more conventional scholarly research. Others claimed my grandfather was trying to monopolize the biographical research on Emily Dickinson by not sharing her dibble.

Grandfather was halfway through writing his massive 600,000 word tome on Emily Dickinson when he first met the girl who later became my grandmother. He was invited to Swarthmore College to speak about Dickinson (a version of this lecture was later published as "Engendered Species: The Polymorphic Bestiary of Emily Dickinson's Secret Life," New Eden Quarterly, 1935).

After his lecture he was approached by a young woman, Abigail Wentworth, whose resemblance to the one existing photograph of Emily Dickinson, age 19, was uncanny.

"Is it certain, Professor Lovejoy," Abigail inquired, "that none of the erotic verses Emily Dickinson wrote to Judge Otis P. Lord are still in existence?"

"The dibble is very clear on this," explained my grandfather. "Every one of those letters was destroyed by Judge Otis P. Lord's daughter on May 15th, 1886 – unbeknownst to her, the very day of Emily Dickinson's death. Perhaps it was simple coincidence that it happened that same day, but I think not. There are still many strange mysteries about Emily Dickinson's life yet to be accounted for."

A series of correspondences took place between Abigail and my grandfather. She probed him on points of fact, such as the inconsistency in his findings that Emily Dickinson had spent winters in Montreal coaching girl's basketball between 1852 to 1856, while archival records at Amherst College showed a number of her correspondences addressed from Amherst during those same winters.

"I found that puzzling, too, at first," agreed my grandfather. "But it's not inconceivable Emily postdated those correspondences and had her sister Lavinia mail them during her absence. We can only speculate at her motives for doing so, but one mustn't doubt the dibble."

What my grandmother saw in my grandfather – thirty-two years her senior, a controversial and malodorous scholar – to agree to be his wife is no more clear than what became of the collection of porcelain clown figurines Emily Dickinson collected over the last two decades of her life.

"Mysteries abound," my grandfather used to say as he waved the wondrous dibble. "One does not need eyes to penetrate the dark if one lights the way with creative intuition and supernatural powers."

My grandfather and grandmother were married. A year later *A Dibbled Identity: The Extraterrestrial Emily Dickinson* was published to great, but short lived, notoriety. And although over the next several decades many inaccuracies were found in my grandfather's text, there are still accounts, such as Emily Dickinson's trembling, orgasmic rapture beneath the fiery tail of Halley's Comet, that are known facts today, thanks to the dibble, despite never actually taking place during Emily Dickinson's lifetime.

The Cello Garden

If music be the food of love, play on:
Give me excess of it, that, surfeiting,
The appetite may sicken and so die.
That strain again! It had a dying fall...

William Shakespeare, TWELFTH NIGHT

The violins were coming up nicely and the basses had just begun to sprout. The French horns were already in full bloom and the timpani looking very robust. There was a promising row of bassoons this year (thank God, after meager harvests the last two years) and I was rather proud of my piccolos and flutes. Many times in the past I'd won competitions for both – blue ribbons, nonetheless – and it looked like this year's crop would be unfailing. What concerned me, though, were the cellos.

I had watered thoroughly – not too much – and applied plenty of nitrogen-rich manure, but the cellos were just not growing. They hadn't even broken through the loose, well-tilled soil. I dug a little to make sure the seeds were not stolen by birds or, perhaps, a rival orchestral gardener, but they were still there, nestled silently within the procreant earth. They just refused to grow, crack out of their embryonic carapace and reach upward toward air and light. My cellos were being stubborn this year and I was not sure why. In all my years as a gardener of orchestras, a conductor of acoustic agronomy, nothing like this had ever happened. The worst had been those two years of meager bassoon growth I mentioned. But for an entire cello section to refuse to grow – this was quite puzzling.

I consulted manuals, almanacs, compositions and compendiums. I studied the notes left behind by Beethoven and Bach, Mozart and Mendelssohn, to see if any of these great symphonic harvesters had come across similar incidents. But I found nothing helpful. The cello, it seems, was always a reliable instrument, a hardy, prodigious instrument. Some even call it the zucchini of orchestral vegetation. I finally put the books asides and went to see my friend Irving.

Irving Leibowitz, a Russian immigrant Jew. A virtuoso with string vegetation, of course. All those Russian Jews were practically born with a bow-stem in their hands. It was Irving who provided the seeds – originally brought over from the Ukraine – for my basses, my violas, my violins, and my cellos.

Irving lived in an apartment complex on the West Side. He'd grown partially deaf and his fingers were hooked and stiff from rheumatism. He received Social Security and a small pension from the city orchestra where he'd played violin for twenty-three years. He'd lived here for fifteen years, after moving from his house in Treble Park shortly after the death of his wife Inanna, or Anna, as she was known.

I tried to visit whenever I could but orchestral gardening is a full-time job. There were also my students at the university to attend to. And, in order to stay in the good graces of the widowed dean, I was giving her hopelessly inept daughter, Chloe, private violin tutelage twice weekly. At best, I saw Irving perhaps once every three months. Usually I found him sitting in silence, his tabby cat, Stradivarius, seated on his lap, his hooked fingers steadily stroking Strad's speckled fur.

On this visit, however, Irving was up and slowly moving around the apartment with a watering can. He had a little pot of harmonicas growing beside the sofa and a window box full of penny whistles. On the fireplace mantel was a vase of freshly cut recorders set beside a photograph of Anna when she was a young woman, when she had first arrived in America.

Those had been heady days for Irving and Anna. He liked to reminisce about them and I was always happy to hear stories about that time in American life when the streets were alive and mellifluous with the sounds of many nations, when the young men from Europe were eager to start careers and families in America, The New World, as Dvorak had dubbed it. Irving arrived with his new bride, a pocket full of seeds and hope for a better life.

"Nathaniel," Irving greeted me, setting his watering can beside the open door. He took my hand with his stiff fingers and led me into the apartment. "Glad to see you. Today is a special day for Stradivarius and myself. It's the anniversary of my marriage to Anna."

There was a weighty photo album on the coffee table he'd pulled out for the occasion. He showed me pictures of their early years together in America. A photo of Anna and him seated with Irving Berlin. Another of them both walking down West Avenue with a young Arthur Fiedler. One of Anna planting a kiss on Benny Goodman's forehead. He pointed out a nightclub photo of Louis Armstrong, cheeks puffed out, blowing a trumpet.

"That's one of mine," he said, full of pride. "I grew it just for Sachmo."

I was impressed, having thought of Irving all these years as only a gardener of string quartets.

"My heart is with the strings," he told me, "but I had a bit of a brass thumb too in those early years and grew some fine, fine trumpets, cornets and trombones. Much later in life I concentrated solely on the strings. I was experimenting even back then, crossbreeding violas and harps, basses and lyres. From those early experiments I developed my first theories of dominant verses recessive acoustics."

I read many of his articles published in the Music Harvesters Almanac and other periodicals, and was familiar with a number of his theories. He was a true musical pioneer, the Gregor Mendel of musicology.

After hearing his remembrances for a while, and imbibing a hearty glass of *slivovitz* or two, I brought up the subject of my cellos, how they were not coming up this year.

"Is that so?" said Irving.

I went on to express my worry and fears of a failed cello crop. Irving averted his eyes, shrugged his shoulders and said, "It may be nothing; just give them more time." He got up from the sofa and moved toward the door where he'd left his watering can.

"Listen Nate," he said, carrying the can into the kitchen, "if they don't take, I'll compensate you as best I can."

This was a ridiculous statement for him to make. I knew Irving had little money and that his retirement benefits were recently reduced due to some fraudulent investments with the city orchestra's pension funds. But Irving felt a certain obligation in the matter since it was he who gave me the seeds for this year's cello crop, as he had done every year previously.

In late March, seeds were handed over without a word of changes he'd made. But now, confronted about my situation, Irving confessed he had given me a new strain of seed. He believed they would improve upon previous harvests.

I had my doubts, but what was I to do? I let the issue drop and decided to wait and see what emerges from the garden.

We had perhaps the worst storm I remember in many years. It was marvelous and horrific all at once, like a Wagner symphony. Thunder rumbled and crashed like mammoth cymbals. Lighting shot down from the tenebrous sky. The whole town trembled. Power lines burst open in live-wire sparks. Many homes were damaged in the storm. Two caught fire and burned completely to the ground. A dozen or so people were injured and three died in accidents said to be related to the storm. One had been a neighbor of mine, Mrs. DaCapo, an elderly patron of the arts, who'd come to her untimely end when the Steinway grand she was hiding beneath collapsed.

I went outside the morning after the storm to clear fallen branches and check for damage. There was nothing much to speak of – a few loose roof cymbals and a fallen trellis of piano keys. I wandered out back to the garden, a bit panicked over what I might find. I was relieved, though, to see the garden remained pretty well intact, except for a couple partially uprooted xylophones.

Then I saw the row where I'd planted the cellos. There were sprouts! At last! I was overjoyed and relieved. I began looking forward, at last, to the autumn when I would have a complete orchestra growing in my garden, perhaps my finest ever.

Things did not turn out exactly as planned. But, like any good gardener, I try to make allowances for the unexpected. The trouble was still with my cellos still. They began to grow – oh yes – but not quite the way my previous cellos had grown. They were thin, nearly flat. I tapped one and heard just a dull melonous thump, instead of the hollow ring I expected. I feared this year's entire cello crop would have to be dug up and turned under.

I blamed Irving and I was angry. *He had switched seeds on me! Experimenting!* when he, himself, knew that so much rested upon my garden, that I could ill afford to take such a risk. It was certainly far too late in the year to replant. My autumn orchestral season would be ruined without my cello section. And Irving was solely responsible.

I avoided confrontation for some time. I did not call or visit Irving all summer. Then unexpectedly, Irving, who rarely makes phone calls, rang me. Perhaps he knew already about the cello business, because his voice sounded a bit hesitant, full of sheepish culpability.

"Nate, my friend, how are things? Well I hope. And the garden? Is everything coming up alright?"

I could not contain my anger, especially after just coming from the garden where I saw, plain as day, the cellos sprouting baroque flourishes of thorny vines, their rotund shells dull and pitted with abrasions. They looked entirely unplayable.

"Irving, I can't believe you would do this to me. I've been your friend for so long. I always trusted and admired you. But you – you know how important the garden is to me. A whole season of Mendelssohn and Dvorak and Tchaikovsky and Vivaldi is scheduled. Advance season tickets already sold. And here you give me these 'seeds', these impossible seeds that have totally thrown off the stability of my harvest. Irving, why would you do such a cheap thing?"

Oh, I was angry. I wasn't even interested in whatever flimsy explanation Irving might offer. I just wanted to vent an entire spring and summer's worth of fury and frustration into the plastic receiver of my phone.

"I know you can't afford to reimburse me for my cellos, Irving. There really isn't any possible way to repair the damage done. The best I can hope is that City College over-watered again and the Philharmonic's *Carmen* gets overrun by gypsy moth. Oh, this is a mess. The worst mess I've been in in years. Not a single cello worth a damn. I might as well pull out the whole damn lot and turn it to compost."

Irving said not a word during my tirade, listening stoically to it all, but suddenly his voice cried in panic.

"No, don't!"

Pleading with me, he continued, "Nathaniel, please don't. Promise me you won't pull out the cellos before they've ripened. I'll do what I can to make it up to you. Just do me this one favor and let them be. I beg you."

My anger subsided beneath his despondency. I reminded myself about all Irving had done for me over the years – the seeds, the sage advice. His intentions were never malicious – though, I confess, there was a time when such subterfuge would not have been entirely unexpected.

You see, I alone perhaps had more to do with the death of Irving's wife, Anna, than any other person.

Let me explain a thing or two about Anna, before I say much more. I had never met Anna Leibowitz, but had seen her play on occasion. She was a gifted cellist

– there's no denying that – but in my opinion she'd made some dreadful choices; she took a beautiful, refined instrument and turned it into a bellows of dread, of mutated sound and discordant, a-rhythmic – well, *noise*, really.

I was fresh out of the conservatory and becoming known for my astute concert and phono-graft reviews. I had several pieces already published in Music Harvesters Almanac, as well as the Agro-Audio Review and Instruments Digest. When Music Harvesters asked me to review the premier of Anna Leibowitz's new solo performance, I leapt at the chance, especially knowing she'd spent the previous two years in seclusion working on what was supposed to be the crescendo of her career, a performance of her own composition titled *Eleusis: The Unspeakable Mysteries*.

Mind you, all this was well before I'd ever met Irving – though I was certainly aware of his work also.

In short, *The Unspeakable Mysteries* turned out to be *unlistenable*, as well. Half the audience left even before intermission. I stayed only because I had a review to write, though I must confess I stopped paying attention at some point. The jumble of shifting Phrygian scales and tumultuous double stopping vanquished all lyricism. The percussiveness of her erratic *col legno* bowing dented and contorted all tempo. The animal-like screeches reverberating from the cello's corpus – well, they gave me chills of horror. I was frightened by the brutality, the violence of her music, its carnality. Such playing was a tense, sustained, neck-breaking game where art danced self-destructively along the rim of impossibility. God knows what she was trying to prove up there, but in a single performance she destroyed what until then had been an impeccable and admirable career.

It is true my review was a bit harsh, giving no mention of her technical mastery or, shall we say, her sheer physical endurance. I also failed to point out the somewhat innovative tonalities and techniques she incorporated, which a few contemporary performers have now adopted. But I was young and full of brass and truly aghast at what she had subjected her audience to.

There were no repeat performances. Nothing more was ever mentioned of *The Unspeakable Mysteries*. And nine months later Anna Leibowitz walked into the ocean, her dress pockets heavy with stones, immersing herself in eternal silence.

Irving, when we finally met two years later at a symphony benefit, seemed to bear no grudge against me. My review of his wife's concert was never brought up. In fact, it was Irving who encouraged me on that very evening to take up orchestral farming.

"Follow your heart's desire," Irving told me, "Cultivate your appetites."

He promised seeds to get me started and told me of other farmers who'd be glad to help. The next spring I moved to a ten-acre estate, suitable for planting. And it's been a successful enterprise ever since.

Until, that is, the trouble with my cellos.

It's a tradition. Every harvest season students from the university come help take in my crop. Afterwards I prepare a huge feast at which we gorge ourselves on sonance, playing upon the cornucopia of my new harvest. Irving – who'd been to my home only once before, the day he brought my first seeds – well, Irving showed up unexpectedly. I was delighted to have him, though, especially to show him first-hand the rotted, gnarled, a-tonal fruition of his ungodly seeds.

"Well, there they are," I said, acerbically, pointing to the menacing crop. The cellos were black as pitch, their necks as thin as corn stalks, their distended bellies raw and bristled, and their strings sharp as thorns. He said not a word, but kept his eyes fixed upon them.

It was then that one of my students, Chloe, the untalented daughter of the dean, entered the cello patch. Other students were diligently gathering up the violins and violas. Cords of brass horns were stacked neatly inside the storage shed. Woodwinds were being hosed off at the side of the house beneath the piano trellis. It was getting dark – rain clouds threatening a storm – and I urged them to hurry and leave the cellos behind.

I was about to walk over, remind Chloe of this, when Irving grabbed my sleeve, pulling me back. Chloe, gripping a bow she'd plucked from its vine, drew forth a long, vociferous moan from one of the deformed cellos.

The other students dropped what they were doing to see the source of these strange emanations. An untended garden hose flooded the lawn. Two flashlights turned upon her lone figure, squatting in the garden, legs astride the black-shelled cello. Chloe was absorbed in playing, head arched back revealing the long white column of her neck.

The strings sobbed and shivered, gradually building into a series of rising intervals, whole tones followed by semi tones. Then came an earthly rumble that, for a moment, seemed an extension of her playing, but gradually became discernible as an approaching storm.

Winds picked up as her playing took on more frantic gestures. Chloe lowered her head revealing features now dark and narrow, eyes reflecting light the way transfixed nocturnal animals often do. These were the features of Anna Leibowitz that had stayed in my mind for so many years. And this, yes, this was the same intense, cacophony Anna Leibowitz conjured many years before.

The sky cracked open with brilliant exclamations of light and thunder. Rain hailed down. Students hurried to gather the last of the instruments, bringing them indoors. And Leibowitz, the old man, nearly deaf, with withered hands, dropped to his knees. And from his eyes poured bitter tears of adoration.

Game Theory for Beginners

We were dating for almost four months before Linnea worked up the nerve to ask. "Would you like to play Canasta with me?"

She was rinsing soapsuds off her dinner plate as she spoke. She tried to make it sound casual, like it just occurred to her. But I could tell by the way her eyes were fixed on her soapy hands she was nervous.

"Okay," I said. "But you'll have to show me how."

She picked up a towel to dry off, then turned toward me. "You've never played Canasta before? Never? Not with any old girlfriends?"

"No," I said.

"And you really want to try? You don't have to if you don't want."

"No, that's okay. I want to."

A smile spread across her pink cheeks as she leaned forward on the toes of her gym shoes. It was the first time I'd seen her smile like that since four months before when I told her, "Daniel's a fool for cheating on you. He doesn't deserve you."

To be quite honest, I didn't enjoy Canasta at first. I was clumsy. I didn't really know what I was doing. I put down the wrong cards at the wrong time. I miscounted points. There were so many rules that just didn't seem to make sense.

Linnea said there was a deep logic to it all. Games like Canasta are not just created overnight. They evolve. Each rule is an adaptation with the ultimate aim of heightening the competition and binding players together in a sort of cooperative opposition.

There is a menacing aspect to Canasta, too, the way it takes over your life and crowds out all other thoughts and sensation. While attending classes, I kept an Italian Canasta deck in my pocket, a totem that I distractedly fondled all day, wearing down the corners with the tip of my thumb. I could barely concentrate on lectures. The overhead projections of distribution channels and utility matrices were drowned out by daydreams of Linnea shuffling decks together, dealing with thumb and index finger, laying down pure melds, dirty melds, stop cards, red threes, wild cards, Canastas.

When classes were over, I'd go to Linnea's place in Neukölln, let myself in and wait for her to come home from her temporary office jobs. I passed the time shuffling cards, fanning them out, reshuffling, waiting for her. When she came through the door, she'd drop her backpack, throw off her purple suede jacket and join me at the kitchen table, on the bedroom floor, at the sofa and coffee table – wherever I had the cards laid out.

While together, we never left the apartment without a Canasta deck. We'd play on the grass in Tiergarten park, on plastic tables outside Kreuzberg kebab stands, on wet Neukölln bar counters, or the sugar sticky Formica of Friedrichstraße café tables. On weekends, if we were at a party together, we'd sometimes slip off to the toilet or spare bedroom for a quick hand or two.

It all came to a cruel end though when Linnea was

awarded a scholarship to go study in the US.

"Why don't you come with mc?" she said.

"What would I do in the US?"

"You could work on your English."

That was about all I could do though. My English was not very good at the time, not good enough to find work or take classes. Socially I would be cut off, not knowing anyone in New York – unlike Linnea, who spent seven years there as a child. In New York, I would become nothing more than her personal Canasta slave. It was clear to us both I would not be going.

The day before Linnea left for America, we played one final game of Canasta. We could barely see well enough through our swollen eyes to count the points at the end of each round.

When she was gone, I didn't quite know what to do with myself. I tried Solitaire, but made me feel all the more alone. I took a part time evening job as a waiter at Hönggerbergs, serving beer and brauts. It helped occupy my time.

"Dear Toby," she wrote, "Life in New York is wonderful. I have a really great professor who teaches a course in game theory. It's all quite a revelation to me. He thinks I should do my thesis on Canasta."

She tried to explain her ideas, how Canasta differs from traditional game theory. In Canasta you could not only play to win or play to make your opponent lose, but you could also play to help your opponent gain far more points than yourself. This is useful if you are able go out before your opponent has laid down a first Canasta, which then turns all his or her points to negative – a very effective strategy, Linnea added, akin to how global corporations play against developing nations with the help of the World Bank and IMF.

At first, we both wrote every few days, but then her letters became less frequent. She wrote she was "super busy" with studies and had discovered a weekly Canasta league that met in a Chinese donut shop in Greenpoint. The thought of Linnea playing four-handed Canasta with complete strangers sickened me. I wrote back I was saving money to come visit over the summer.

"That would be great," she replied. "I miss you."

Not long after that she wrote again, telling me it might not be such a good idea to come. Her ex-boyfriend Daniel was now working in New York and they had started playing Canasta together again.

I was despondent. I wrote her pleading letters. I would come to America and we would talk about things. She didn't respond. I started mailing cards. Every day I sent a two of hearts. I sent her fifteen twos, a full hand, before I finally received a response. It was a black three, the stop card.

I tried to move on with my life. I had several dates with other students. Each seemed to go worse than the previous. Any time I broached the subject of Canasta I received strange looks. One girl, Magda, never heard of Canasta. I tried to explain. She wrinkled her nose as if smelling something offensive and said, "That sounds really weird."

I placed a personal ad in *Berliner Zeitung* looking for a Canasta partner. My first response was a 50-year-old clerk at the Deutsche Bahn named Heinrik who was also a fanatic about Pachisi and Risk. I didn't bother to write him back.

When I had almost given up hope, I received a letter from Elzbieta, a linguistics student from Wroclaw, Poland. She had had a little Canasta experience while working as a nanny in London. She was interested in exploring it more deeply.

Elzbieta was not bad for a Canasta novice. She knew her way around a deck of cards, shuffling and fanning with the fluidity of a professional. I liked the way she bit her bottom lip, concentrating as she dealt.

"That's only thirteen," I said after she'd finished dealing. "We each need two more cards."

"It will be easier for me if we play by British rules," she said, laying down the deck and giving me a penetrating stare.

I began learning new British rules with each round. By the fourth round she had laid down two what she called "half Canastas" and one "wet meld." A couple turns later, she tried to pull a previously discarded ace from the middle of the discard pile.

"It was my ace," she said. "You can do that in British rules."

I was becoming a bit skeptical about these British rules, but I did not say anything. I let Elzbieta appropriate my three of hearts with her duplicate three, build a "Royal Canasta" from a mixture of red face cards, then use her one-eyed Jack for what she called a "capture" card. I let her go on and on showing me surprising new rules and kicking my ass in the process. I didn't mind though. I was learning a lot. Elzbieta perhaps was not as artful or subtle a player as Linnea, but I was beginning to understand the theory behind the game.

Maurice Utrillo

If there is a place to start, it's not at a doorway, it's not on a sheet of parchment or primed canvas. If there is a place to start, it's with a wall, blanched whiter than white, so white it's almost not even there, a vacancy in the landscape, a missing piece of town.

Maurice shouldered his way past the crowd and stood before the wall so that it filled his peripheral vision and the whole town became a wall for him. And as he peered closely, he saw that the vast white expanse was not truly a vacancy, but a place unto itself, with its embossed craters, lips of mortar, imbricated veins of brush stokes layered like intersecting pathways. He saw the gradient shades that hadn't been there in the distance. He saw the minuscule shadows of its pitted surface, the faint persimmon corners of plastered-over brick, the verdant spores of lichen, the trace deposits of dirt, ash and ecru bird droppings.

His eyes wandered the wall in exploration. Here was a place to start again. The cravings in his veins, like an army of red ants, slowed their march to a halt as the wall absorbed his entire attention. He did not think about another glass, another smoke, another night alone. He did not think about the garden of cherry trees, flowering bougainvillea and crocuses that lay just beyond the wall's cap of shattered glass embedded in mortar. Nor did he think of the town hall, the breeze bearing up the stripes of the flag. Nor of the town and its people, its ridicule and gossip. Nor of his mother and his drinking companions. Only the wall, which was absolute yet yielding to so many suggestions. He ran his hand along its braided surface. It scraped against his palm and fingertips. There was depth here that could not be recognized from a distance. How was one to convey this, to explain it?

He would need to work fast. If he hurried home and got his paints he might still capture the wall in this light and be able to reproduce its expanse and the suggested possibilities it conveyed to him at that moment. If he hurried. If he walked quickly. If he passed the café and no one spoke his name. If the Russian waitress, Irina, did not call out to him. If Monsieur Henri did not accost him for payment. If his blood stayed calm and the vision of white stayed before him and did not leave him for one moment.

The Brain Harvest

It was later summer, the start of the brain harvest. The temporary workers – many having crossed the border from Mexico, leaving family and friends behind – were out in the fields hacking brains from the vines and stacking them into the back of sun-faded Ford pick-ups, ready to be rushed off to universities in time for fall classes. I had been hitchhiking across the country and managed to get a job working the harvest in order to earn enough money to keep on moving on with my grinding, peripatetic approach toward San Francisco, my final destination. I had friends there who were straight and clean, and I could stay with them for a time while I tried to get my life back on track.

I had no idea what tough work brain harvesting could be. We started in the 5 a.m. morning chill and worked as the sun rose and sucked the land dry. Laboriously, we disentangled vines, pulling weeds, yanking out the stubborn, green and silver haired brain pods, whacking them clean from the vine with machetes and carrying them – often through thick, foot-clinging irrigation mud – to the back of trucks where someone else would arrange them into orderly stacks, like cut timber. Then came lunch, when we were driven to the mess tent and ladled out some weak broth, along with beans and rice, tortillas and sometimes a well bruised apple. Then it was back to the fields to reap more brains.

The Mexicans were all veterans of this sort of work and went about their harvesting silently, efficiently, without complaint. For me, though, it was agony. My feet blistered. My hands were scratched raw from the prickly vines that needed to be pulled loose to get to the brains. After a couple days, some of the scratches became infected.

"*Eso se ve doloroso*," said Consuala, a beautiful Mexican girl from San Cristóbal. She took pity on my red swollen palms. Holding them delicately between her small hands, she examined them carefully. One of the cuts was leaking a soapy green fluid.

"No good," she said in English. The tops of her own hands were smooth, unblemished brown skin. Underneath, though, were layers of dark calluses from two seasons of brain harvesting and four years of embroidering logos in a *maquiladora* factory for Fruit of the Loom.

That evening Consuala made a salve by boiling plants she called "*Flores d muerto*," death flowers. She rubbed the oily pulp into my wounds then carefully wrapped my palms with strips of cloth generously torn from the bottom of one of her three t-shirts. She offered up a prayer to Ixtlilton, the Aztec god of the brain harvest, then piously waved the Christian Sign of the Cross in the air between us.

Consuala assured me this would not only heal my hands but strengthen my heart.

"My heart is fine," I said. "*Mi corazón es bueno*. It's my hands that are all fucked up."

With these repairs I was able to continue with the harvest, but could still not quite keep pace with the Mexicans. The foreman, himself a Mexican, had no patience for me. *Gringo perezoso!* He spat insults in

Spanish behind my back.

"Go home Yankee," he jeered, then laughed riotously at his own not-so-clever use of English.

Señor Penelou muttered something under his breath that made the others laugh. But neither I, nor the foreman, understood. It was in a native Indian dialect, not Spanish.

"*¡Más trabajo y menos charla!*" yelled the foreman.

None of them could comprehend what I, an American citizen, was doing taking jobs away from Mexican mestizos, the only truly skilled and rightful workers for handling brain harvests. Undoubtedly, it seemed, they were right, because my hands and feet could not keep up. And when, eventually, my bowels couldn't either, I had no choice but to quit the harvest early, meaning I could not collect the money I had already earned over the previous ten days of torturous labor.

There was no easy way out for me. I had only three dollars and forty-seven cents. My jeans were mud splattered. The bandages around my hands were dirty. I stank probably worse than I could even imagine. I had only one clean shirt, but at least I had that.

"Goodbye, Consuala," I said, kissing her on the forehead beneath the arrow-straight part of her shining black hair. "Tomorrow I go. Wish me luck."

"I say prayer for you, *Señor* Paul."

On my last day, I managed to slip a couple brains behind the bushes near the row of plastic outhouses. That night, with my few belongings strapped to my back, I snuck out of my tent, pulled the two brains from beneath the deerweed, climbed the fence and headed toward the wide black freeway.

It was all a matter of luck that one of those brains

turned out to have a great facility for handling numbers and the other a miraculous gift of precognition.

Once in Nevada, I managed to use the two brains to gather up staggering sums of money gambling in casinos. Night after night, we worked our way up from the south, doing mainly roadside hotels and small town nightclubs. The Sandman. The Wigwam. Kitty's Club. Slot World. Castaways. Jackpot 51. The Holster Club. And dozens of others.

"Double it," I told the croupier at the Pyramid.

The fat man in the green polyester suit beside me removed the cigar nib from his purple bottom lip and gave me a murderous glare. The busty brunette on his arm grinned and blinked her long black lashes at me. The brains hummed inaudibly within my duffle bag. The croupier, with vacant eyes and colorless lips, moved my chips on top of the nine. For once in my life everything was all too easy.

I eventually did make it to San Francisco to see my friends. They were worried, not having heard from me in months.

"We thought you were lost," said Claire as she laid Indian saris and Navajo blankets over the futon where I would sleep. "We weren't sure how to reach you. Tomorrow Richard is going to set you up with a Yahoo! email account."

"Will you be able to find me with that?" I asked. I'd heard of email, but wasn't sure how it was supposed to reach me without a computer.

"We've got some catching up to do," she said in reply. "San Francisco is a completely different world compared to Providence. I think this is where all the lost souls end up finding a home."

I wasn't planning to make a home for myself in San Francisco, though. Especially not just then. I had the two brains and I wanted to keep using them, keep winning, keep amassing the money they earned me.

When the weekend was over, I thanked Claire and Richard. Said I would keep in touch. Then took off.

I took the brains to some sad little Indian reservations in Mendocino and then up toward Eureka. We made out well in those places. I didn't feel guilty about cleaning them out. Those reservation Indians seemed as fixated on taking people's money as I was in winning it.

After a few weeks playing these small time casinos, the brains felt ready for some larger prospects. We barreled our way down Highway 5 in a white AMC Javelin I'd won at a private card party in Dunsmuir. In Sacramento, we hit Highway 80 and headed straight through the night toward the desert gold of Nevada.

I spent two years traveling like that. I was no longer driving the Javelin, though, nor the Porsche 911 I'd won after that, but a yellow two-seater Mercedes SL500 convertible. My wheels were my one ostentatious showing. Other than that, I dressed in nondescript street clothes and stayed in budget motels. I had the money for nicer places, deluxe accommodations, suites, penthouses... But the amenities were wasted on me. I wasn't there to enjoy myself, relax, sit by the pool, indulge in gourmet dining. I thought only about winning. Not wealth. Not luxury. Just simple, uncomplicated, quantifiable sums of cash.

Then one of those weird twists of fate happened that dispel everything you'd ever thought was right, unraveling the path beneath your feet so that the once solid pavement suddenly seems like a precarious thread you're balancing upon. I was staying at the Motel 8 outside of Saint George. I had just gathered up my things, ready to move on, when the cleaning lady knocked.

Her arms were full of white linens. She was startled to see me.

"*Señor* Paul. *¿Qué esta haciendo usted aquí?*"

I didn't recognize her at first. Money had towered over the past, obscured it in shadow. But then something clicked together like a row of double cherries in the slots and I remembered her soft voice and the taste of her warm, saliferous brow against my lips. It was Consuala, the Mexican girl I had known from the brain harvest.

She asked me to hold up my hands like she was robbing me at gunpoint. Then I realized she wanted only to see my palms and how they'd healed. I'd forgotten all about those scars. She moved closer and examined them like she was reading my fortune. Could she see all the great wealth coming my way? Did those lines and creases shine like veins of gold?

Her finger drew lines upon the vague shadows of scars. She gently took my hands, held them close to her face and breathed in. When she released my palms, she asked only if they still hurt. Inexplicably I cried, cried like I hadn't in years.

At the time, I thought it was an improbable coincidence to see her again, like something out of a novel, not like something that really happens in a person's life. Now, though, after abandoning those brains in the Motel 8 and living with Consuala for many years as husband and wife, raising three beautiful daughters, living a richer, fuller life than I had ever known, I can look back at everything that has happened to me, everything that seemed to defy the odds, and realize the world has more to show and tell us than all the brains ever harvested will ever be able to explain.

Making Babies

My girlfriend Annie wanted to make babies. The week before it was stained glass window ornaments. The week before that it was homemade bread. A month ago it was an indoor herb garden. I don't know where she gets these ideas. Probably from women's magazines. Anyway, I'm game for anything that will keep her busy and make her happy. And, really, how hard can making babies be? Certainly not as friggin' difficult as layering colored sand and pebbles at the bottom of a decorative terrarium.

"It will be easy and fun. You'll see," said Annie in the same fatal words that the painfully complex instructions for soldering glass pebble jewelry began.

Annie, it's true, can be a bit capricious. But she is at least methodical in her caprice. She began spending lunch hours at Barnes & Noble, browsing the *Parenting & Family* section (oddly situated between *New Age & Occult* and *Pets*). Credit card in hand, she charged up a stack of books and periodicals that could tower over even the tallest of toddlers. Every evening for the next two weeks we perused the baby making materials while sitting on the sofa, watching action movies on DVD and hefty doses of reality TV.

One evening Annie set down her copy of *Prenatal Care for Dummies* and said to me, "I'm ready to try some of this stuff. What do you think?"

"Maybe after the movie, Hon."

But there is no putting Annie off once she has an idea fixed in her head. Before you knew it we were heavily into "You Name It!" Chapter Four of *Pathways to Parenthood.*

"How 'bout Charlene?" I suggested.

"No. Hold on," Annie said. "You can't just call out names. We have to subscribe to the baby name internet newsletter or buy the pack of baby name selector cards."

I pointed out that the *Rough Guide to Babies* suggested drawing appellation inspiration from telephone books, dictionaries and world atlases, provided you followed the guidelines in column seven of table 12E in the appendix. So we tried that and basically came up with the names *Sagamore* if it's girl or *Thrombosis* if it's a boy.

We pretty much disregarded the following chapter, *Feng Shui for the Nursery.* Not simply because it involved buying a lot of stuff we didn't have the money for, but it also required having a spare room not filled to the gills with stained glass, soldering equipment, bread pans, top soil, Styrofoam cylinders, glass beads, button makers, unpainted ceramic figurines and the detritus of various other hobbies and projects not yet completed.

"Can't we just jump ahead to the good stuff?" I urged.

So we skipped over the financial planning chapter and the guidelines on nutrition and exercise and plunged right into the creative visualization.

"Concentrate solely on your breathing," Annie read. "Feel the air enter your body and fill every pore and cell from the tip of your fingers down to your toes. Gently expel the air, relaxing muscles as the breath gradually leaves your body."

Muscles in my shoulders and neck that I didn't know were clenched suddenly gasped air and released their stranglehold. I became so calm I barely noticed the TV docudrama *Sex Slave: The Secret Life of Tony Blair* had ended and the late news had begun. I kept my eyes shut, listening to Annie's voice as she continued reading. "Deep within every cell of your body lies a little black box containing a genetic blue print. Picture that box slowly opening. Then, with your palms down and knees shoulder width apart…"

I must have drifted into a deep, deep slumber at that moment, because all I remember is a little version of myself, completely hairless and naked, floating freely in space, swimming in a black sea of stars and galactic nebula. My tiny, bulbous limbs spun and paddled as I maneuvered my cherubic flesh in arcs and dives, my small toothless mouth open wide, swallowing the sequins of starlight and the streams of luminescent gasses rising from the quivering pink topography below with its teeming rivers of blood and salient adipose hillsides.

There was tranquility and quiet like I had never known. I had never heard quiet before, didn't even know it had its own sound, a melody, really, that moved like a leaf upon the water's surface, slowly flowing and spinning.

Suddenly, there was a disturbance, a disruption in the melodic quiet, two voices calling out from nowhere, calling to me.

"Thrombosis," they said. That's not really my name, but I knew they were calling me. "Thrombosis, come to us. Come here."

The voices cried sweetly, imploringly.

"We want you here beside us. Thrombosis, come."

But all I could think was, "No. Please. Let me stay just where I am. Just here. Where I am."

The Last

We ran out of nails and were using duct tape, extension cords, wedged chairs, cabinet doors, the torn braids of floor rugs – anything we could think of to keep the windows sealed and the doors blocked. There were thuds on the rooftop. A clattering in the attic. The creak of nails pried loose. Wood panels splintering. Glass windowpanes cracking. Cold drafts rushing in from between the boards we'd hastily secured in place.

They had caught scent of us, knew we were inside. They repeatedly launched short attacks, then retreated into the trees and tall grass, waiting, watching, seeing if we would make a run for it.

Only three hours before, I had laid Jessica on the kitchen floor, her calves upon my shoulders, lost in the heat of the moment. Garden potatoes roasted in rosemary and extra virgin olive oil. The Wedgewood stove smoked and steamed.

We performed recklessly, passionately, hurriedly. Daniel, her husband, would be home any moment. And not more than ten minutes after we'd zipped, buttoned, snapped, clasped and pinned everything back in place did we hear the tearing bite of gravel as Daniel's Pathfinder came skidding up the drive.

"My God! Holy fucking God!" he cried, the cabin door slamming behind him.

Jessica and I looked at each other, drew in our breaths. How could he know? Did he have the phone line tapped? A private detective perched in the redwood grove? How did he know?

We hurried out of the kitchen and into the main room of their small Mendocino mountain home. Mud was caked upon Daniel's Timberland boots and splattered across his L. L. Bean khakis and white cotton twill sweater. His face was contorted like a warped image in a concave mirror. He was breathing hard; his mouth open, but unable to speak.

"Danny, what is it?"

Jessica hurried to his side. Daniel tossed his brown leather shoulder bag onto the deacon's bench and threw his arms around her.

"I don't even know how to say it."

We turned on the radio. The news reports were like something out of a 1950's science fiction film. I kept thinking it was some new form of entertainment in which the drama – no longer satisfied with the confines of a two dimensional television set – escapes into the real, three-dimensional world.

What we gathered from a barrage of harried and sketchy news reports was that at 12:15 that afternoon a series of explosions went off in major cities along the west coast of the United States, emitting an unidentified cloud of noxious gas. Near ground zero of each explosion, tens of thousands of people dropped dead. As rescue crews came to the scene, the previously dead bodies began to rise and walk again, exhibiting mindless and brutal behavior. Rioting took place, and it was believed more people died in the ensuing violence than were killed in the initial explosions.

The power went off, silencing the radio announcer in mid report.

"Who are you calling?" said Jessica.

"Someone I know at the mayor's office. He ought to know what's going on."

The line was busy. Jessica took the phone from me and tried calling her mother. Before she got through the line went dead.

The three of us stepped onto the porch to survey the surrounding landscape. The sun had just fallen behind the ridge. The mountain's shadow longingly spread along the panorama, darkening the slope, the lichen spotted boulders, motley evergreens, girthsome redwoods, sapling pines and the long emboss of fire trails.

Roughly two hundred yards of road were still visible, descending into the trees and down toward Fort Bragg. Their closest neighbors lived a mile uphill – a 60-year-old marijuana farmer and his 28-year-old girlfriend, a glass blower who created one-of-kind glass dildos for erotic boutiques and quirky art galleries.

"Should we drive up and see what they're doing?" Jessica asked.

We were just getting into the Pathfinder when we saw the couple approaching. They walked slowly. No hurry. No expression of panic. No expression whatsoever. They looked in our direction, but did not return our greetings.

That's how it began. And the rest of the details are too gruesome for me to try and recall at this moment.

Where all the others came from, I don't know. It's not a densely populated area and none of them approached by car or bus – at least as far as I could tell.

We barricaded ourselves inside. Jessica put antiseptic on my left arm, then bandaged the raw and painful bite marks in gauze. Daniel counted up the food stock and figured we had enough to last two weeks. Maybe three. Together, we fashioned weapons out of cutlery, a woodworking kit and some gardening tools. We lit candles and piled more scrap lumber into the hearth as the day grew darker and the room grew cold.

We sat quietly, listening. The yellow glow of the hearth illuminated our hands, necks and faces. Jessica's chest rose and fell with long steady breaths. Warm light flickered upon her skin and flashed against her moist eyes. Her bottom lip hung down, quivering as she stared into the flames.

And – for a dizzy, feverish moment – even with the scratching noises still coming from the attic and the smashing and ripping of the Pathfinder's safety glass, I was willing to risk it all, bringing it all down, the house, the home, the West Coast, and all God's creation, for just one last taste of Jessica's lips.

My Lobotomy

It's hard to even remember a time before my lobotomy, though it only happened several months ago. So much has changed since then. After my release from the ward, I went straight to my family's old summer place in Traverse City to get my head together, so to speak, and figure out what to do with my new life.

My new life. That's what it felt like. A fresh start. No more of the old troubles. They were all diced asunder, along with that troublesome prefrontal gray matter. The doctor told me a lobotomy, or leucotomy, as they prefer to call it nowadays, was like having a colostomy. Part of your intestine goes bad, you snip off the bad part. No worry, because there's plenty more of it, yards and yards all coiled up inside. Human lives are replete with redundancy.

While I was in Traverse City, I fell in love. Well, at least I think I fell in love. We were fucking a lot and talking about marriage and kids, so it pretty much must have been love. Her name was Gloria, Gloria Martino. Her father was a business tycoon who'd made his fortune selling plastic air conditioning vents to the auto industry.

Gloria hadn't told me she was already married. If she had, I'd forgotten. It wasn't an issue until the day her husband showed up at my door. I answered, still in my pajamas.

"Are you Jason Kavenaugh Junior?" asked the man. I noticed the silver nub of a Derringer handgun pointed at my stomach.

"No, I'm not," I said. "He left a few months ago. Haven't seen him since."

The man had tremendous eyebrows, the size of nail scrubbers. They slanted together as his forehead collapsed into deep furrows of concentration.

After a moment, he relaxed his shoulders, lowered the gun and said, "Okay."

Before turning away, he added, "If he comes back tell him Lou Martino came looking for him. Got that? Lou Mar-ti-no."

I nodded and thought how unlike Gloria this man seemed. I could hardly imagine this dark-haired Mediterranean-looking fellow being Gloria's brother, father or any close relation.

Later that day, Gloria called and shed some light on the situation. "That was my husband Lou," she said. "He found out about us and came looking to kill you."

Even with a good portion of my cortex cut loose, I knew enough to get out of town quickly before Lou came back asking more questions. I packed a couple travel bags and went to visit my old college pal Marnie in Miami.

"Gosh oh geez oh," said Marnie, as I set my bags down in the foyer of the Grand Americana where he lived on 28th floor. "You look just fine. No one would ever guess lookin' atcha what you been through."

"Thanks, Marnie," I said. He lost his smile and looked a bit bewildered.

"Did you just call me Marnie?" he said. "It's Bill."

Then he laughed and punched me hard in the shoulder. "But you knew that. Ha. Ha. Y'er still the same ol' Jaykay. Always joking."

Marnie showed me around Miami and introduced me to the *crème de la crema* of Miami's leisure class. He took me to some great nightclubs where I grew an appreciation for Cuban brass, Havana cigars, salsa dancing and *yucca fritters*. I got involved with a voluptuous and hot-tempered little *señorita* from San Salvador named Ana Maria, or Amy, as she liked to be called. She was a petite woman with sapphire eyes that looked like they could cut glass. Dark brown hair, long as a horse's tail, ran past her waist and dangled playfully upon her little rump.

"Chew know whaz wrong wit chew?" she said one night out in the parking lot of the El Pescadoro. "You no kay make up yo' mind."

She was right about that. Or maybe she wasn't.

I would have married Amy and gotten her that Green Card if it wasn't for Gloria, who I was still maybe in love with, since I didn't remember falling out of love with her – even though none of that really mattered now, because she was already married to some guy who fit cement loafers for the Mafioso. I tried to explain this to Amy.

"Whaz zit wit chew?"

"Excuse me?"

"Aw, no. No no no no no. You no gonna play like you no unde'stand me, Mista."

"But really, Amy, I don't understand what you're saying."

Her handbag swung hard at my face, the clasp scratching my left cheek enough to bleed.

"Whatz da matte' wit chew? You keep tellin' me dis same shit ovah 'n ovah like I'z some kinda reta'ded. What da fuck I ca'e abou' dis Gloria bitch? Eh? An' stop fuckin' callin' me Amy, man."

A few days later, I was having drinks at the One

Eyed Pirate with Amy and her new friend Salvador or Sergio – I forget the name – and I blacked out. When I came to, I was laying in the back seat of a stranger's T-bird convertible. My wallet, traveler's checks, Rolex watch, monogrammed cigarette case and left sock were all gone.

I never saw Amy again after that. But I don't hold any hard feelings. She really did what she had to do in her situation, just as Lou Martino tried to do what he had to do, and Doctor Killbourne, my psychiatrist, did what he had to do, and my parents – God rest their souls – did all they could do.

What we do is who we are and who we are is what we do. It's very simple, isn't it? I really couldn't see it though before my operation. Back then I thought who I was had something to do with what I desired and hoped to be real. Now I see everything that matters just simply is. We're kidding ourselves about inner lives and subconscious brainwaves and stuff like that that never seem to work themselves up to the splashy surface of real conscious action.

It took a good swift severing of my cingulated gyrus from the remainder of my limbic system for me to see that! But now that I have my life is so much better than it could ever possibly have been before. And troubles – they're all just a thing of the past.

Phaedra

My grandfather said to me, "You – at your age – what does a girl your age know about love?" and I was angry with him and all adults for thinking they held a monopoly on real emotions. If that were true, why didn't they live with them more instead of stuffing them in scrapbooks and referring to them only as fond or painful memories? I would like to see for once a living specimen of an adult person in love. Don't read to me out of some book. Don't quote me Pablo Neruda or fuckin' e.e. cummings.

I am still young, I know. But when I was very young, I used to dream of being abducted by a god, taken down to the underworld or up to the upper world, ravaged and held for ransom until some prince or minor deity came to my rescue. And love was somehow bound up in that – the idea of love – that you couldn't just say it, but you had to do something really, really great, something heroic and daring in order to be beloved.

As it turned out, no gods were much interested in ravaging me. And my grandfather's colleagues were more interested in explaining their theories about adolescent female sexuality than actually doing anything more than cornering me at some faculty party and trying to force-feed me verse from Coleridge or Keats as if I suffered from some sort of anorexia of rhyming verse.

My parents figured it was best for me to live in the country with my grandparents than to stay with them in the city. Maybe they thought love could fall and lose itself more easily in all these pine needles and dead leaves. If only that were true. Sometimes, still, my heart feels like a caged animal in my chest, gnawing away at my ribs, and I want only to hold my breath and suffocate it.

Just before the move, my parents took me out of school for a week. I had concussed my head on the toilet in the girl's room. I was doing The Trick again – The Trick, as the other girls called it, trying to pass it off as a cheap stunt. But it was more than just that. A trick is something a hooker did for money or a dog did for biscuits. There was no one dangling any rewards for us. We did it for ourselves, to ourselves.

We held Glad bags to our mouths, sealing the plastic to our glossed lips. We blew in and out, in and out, until all the electrons in our heads drew together into one tiny spot in the center of our foreheads. They'd shimmer there for a bit just before everything disappeared. Everything. The other girls. The bathroom. The faculty. The school. The planet. The universe. Instant Nirvana. All gone. Wiped clean. And when we came to, for a moment, we didn't know where we were or who we were or that we were. It's just all out there. Life. And then slowly, naively we entered back into it.

Downstairs at my grandparents', they were "entertaining" and playing Billy Holiday records on their precious old Magnavox. *Chinks do it. Japs do it. Upper Lapland little Lapps do it.* They were talking about wine again as if that were the only thing they shared in common apart from their jobs at the college.

I could hear it all through the air vents, even

Professor Alvarez's raspy voice as he trotted out, once again, his one little gem of wisdom about how bringing a vine near death brings out its most intense flavor. And I heard and didn't want to hear and wanted it all to go away and for me to go away and I pulled the sheets up over my head and thought about The Trick.

The only plastic bag was a large yellow one that held my lacrosse cleats. So I tried that, gripping it halfway down and holding it tight to my lips. I inhaled the scent of leather, perspiration, dirt and grass. I blew into it, filling the bag. Then I inhaled it all back. Again I repeated this, breathing in and out from the bag, in and out. I continued doing this until there was only that last whisper of Billie Holiday singing.

Baby, you're too lovely
You're much too lovely to last…

When my eyes opened, I couldn't quite make anything out. I didn't know where I was. I could have been lying on a mountaintop. I could have been chained to a rock by the sea. I could have been sprawled across some strange man's dirty sheets. What did it matter? For a moment nothing mattered, because I didn't know where I was or who I was or the *why* and *because* of anything.

And for that brief moment it was almost as if I'd been rescued.

The Habits

She walked her habit into the bar and took a seat at the counter. The bartender wearing a black armband said, *What can I getcha?* as he polished the counter with a wet rag. She ordered her habit a scotch on the rocks, then a mineral water for herself. *Right cha go*, said the bartender and turned to pour the drinks. She rested her hand upon the habit, giving it a gentle squeeze to let it know it would not have to wait much longer.

I've seen her there many times before. I come there often with my own habit (a small one, a good one, really, but you know how habits are). We've never spoken. It's not that kind of bar. People go there with their habits to let them run free for a while, tire themselves out, then bring them home to bed, to drift off into dreams, dreams of long pink finger nails with savory cuticles shaped like Moorish moons, street puddles hungry for rubber boots, wet thumbs glistening like bulbous fruits – whatever it is small habits dream about when not busy trying to become bigger ones.

My habit was on its third mai tai. A strange drink for a habit. A preference picked up years ago from my ex-wife's habit. The little fella was about exhausted. I was anxious to get it home and put it to bed, so I could have just a few moments to myself.

But then something happened that changed everything. A man walked into the bar holding a gun close to his chest. He moved briskly, straight up to the bartender and tersely demanded something. I couldn't hear exactly what. The bartender reached below the cash register. This only made the man angrier. He shouted, "No you don't," raised the gun and shot the bartender in the head.

Everyone froze. It was not what you would have expected. No one moved. No one said anything. Not a single habit stirred. The man with the gun looked at us all, sneered, his face contorting in disgust. He spat on the floor, murmured something inaudible and quickly ran out of the bar.

Then everyone snapped to. They grabbed their jackets, purses and briefcases and quickly fled the bar, fumbling with car keys, hailing cabs, some just running off through the parking lot toward the freeway.

I was on my way out the door when she grabbed my arm.

"Somebody needs to do something," she said.

I was embarrassed for her, for myself, for all of us. I gestured toward the parking lot and said, "I can't. I gotta get home."

But she wouldn't let go of my arm.

"Don't you see?"

She pulled me back into the bar. I looked around and saw all the habits were still there, quietly waiting, drinks set in front of them, curls of dirty gray smoke drifting off lit cigarettes, shredded napkins, twisted hair, heavy sighs. Even my own habit was still there, sucking out the frothy remains of its last mai tai.

"We can't leave them like this," she said. And I saw she was right.

We gathered up all the habits and took them to my

place. I live in a small, two-bedroom home in the Fair Oaks housing development. Hardly a big enough place for so many habits, but we did what we could to make them comfortable.

Priscilla was her name. She stayed the night and, not long afterwards, moved in with me. We devoted ourselves to tending to all the habits. So many of them. And all competing for our attention. It was exhausting.

I'd pretty much given up trying to do anything *but* tend to the habits. It was the same for Priscilla. Weeks passed by without the two of us ever exchanging more than a few words, and those were usually in regard to one habit or another.

At night, I would fall into a long dark tunnel of sleep from which I would not emerge until the first habits of morning cried out for my attention. Priscilla hardly slept at all, though. When she did, she had discomforting dreams. Nightmares really. She grew thin. And pale. And weak. Hardly had the strength any more to keep up with the habits, which meant I had to pick up the slack and take on more and more of them.

One day she said to me, "Josh, do you know what it is I keep dreaming about? I keep dreaming about that man."

"What man?"

"That man. The one who shot the bartender. That night. Did you get a good look at him? I think he was an angel."

That's when I knew Priscilla had reached her breaking point. The habits were too much for her. I drove us to the hospital where she signed all the papers admitting herself. Then I hurried back home. I gathered the habits, loaded them into the car, and we drove off very far that night. Far away.

To nowhere in particular.

The Blue Bedouins

The big problem with the Washtenaw Creative Writing Program was that the instructors kept insisting we write about what we knew. We were nearly all in our early twenties. The dewiness of youth was still slick upon us and hadn't yet fully dissipated into the hot dry air of adult lives. We basically knew nothing and tended to write in a hollow, drowsy prose about drinking sprees, backseat car sex, and the untimely death of family pets.

Professor Tognazzini would hand back our stories, scratch the stubble on his jaw, and mutter things such as, "You poor, normal kids" or "You must have suffered as much writing this as I did reading it" or to me once, "You, Wilson, seem awfully too well adjusted to want to be a writer."

One day Professor Tognazzini came to class looking a little out of sorts – shirt un-tucked, hair stuck up at odd angles, eyes glassy and lower lids puffed out like inverted mushroom caps. Looked like he hadn't slept or bathed in the three days since our last class. I detected a faint scent of bourbon, sweat, and bacon grease when he walked past.

"I give up," he said. "I hadn't wanted to do this, but I see no other choice." He started pointing toward the biggest guys in class. "You. You. Everz. Bridberg. Cismousky. Fuller. Come with me."

After ten minutes, they returned wheeling an enormous piece of machinery. They removed the dollies from underneath and lowered it to the floor. The red painted sides of the machine were nearly Professor Tognazzini's height and approximately twice his width. Thick brown leather straps on both sides held glass cylinders the size of barber shop poles, but somewhat wider. Attached to these cylinders by tarnished fixtures were long clear hoses that ran back and forth along the machine. Professor Tognazzini took one of the two plastic jugs he carried and poured its contents into the funnel atop one glass cylinder.

"I suppose you're wondering what this is," he said, as the clear liquid gurgled its way through the tubes.

He set down the empty container, lifted the second one and continued pouring. A waft of some stringent, yet sweet, smelling chemical spread through the room.

"I found this during my stay in Budapest. Actually, I won it. But that's another story. This, Ladies and Gentleman, is a time machine."

Professor Tognazzini began twisting, poking, and pulling the various switches and levers. Lights went on and soon the machine sputtered and coughed like an enormous percolator.

The class sat silently, filled with a certain apprehension. Perhaps fear. Some of Professor Tognazzini's past experiments with us, such as Gender Bender, Knock Knock and the Name on the Forehead game, had made us a little uneasy. But this seemed very different. Threatening in a way. Like being asked to write down your first sexual experience. Only maybe worse.

Julie Chibarro was the first one called to the front of the class and told to step inside. Professor Tognazzini adjusted levers while the machine steamed, whistled and hummed steadily along. In a few moments, the door re-opened. Chibarro emerged, bright eyed, smiling. There were grass stains on her denim knees that hadn't been there before. Bits of crumpled leaves were caught in her tangled blonde hair.

"Holly shit," Chibarro said. "You wouldn't believe what just happened to me."

She told us a story about living with a North American Indian tribe long before the American colonies were settled and how she had fallen for a particularly hunky young warrior. Her adventure went on for six full weeks, though, in actual time, she'd only been in the machine for no more than a minute of two.

One after another, students came out of the machine with remarkable tales about adventures in other time periods and distant lands. We all had a bit of a fright at one point when the door opened and Karl Koerner failed to re-appear. Professor Tognazzini shut the door, readjusted some settings, kicked it a couple times, and Karl eventually tumbled out amidst a flurry of cherry blossoms. He'd been living in Feudal Japan for six years and was hard-torn over whether or not to return.

As it neared my turn to enter the machine I grew increasingly nervous. I wasn't sure I liked the idea of time travel. What was wrong with the here and now? What was wrong with writing about my dog? I loved that dog, damnit. Yet everyone else in class seemed to enjoy their time travel. And all had returned with surprising experiences to tell. No one, fortunately, had been dropped behind hostile enemy lines in the midst of battle. No one returned mortally wounded or infected with plague. Laura Conway had found herself in a Guiana refugee camp and there was not much pleasantness about that. But she was only there for twenty-four hours and during that time she had helped raise spirits by teaching the women Appalachian folk songs and the Name on the Forehead game.

When it was finally my turn, I bent my head, entered the machine, and sat stoop-shouldered upon a small metal stool, waiting for the world to change. The seat vibrated beneath me. The mechanical humming made my ears ring. A minute passed and nothing happened. Two minutes. Was something wrong? I shut my eyes and clenched my teeth. I tried to think what might happen. A picture slowly formed in my mind, becoming increasingly vivid as I focused inward.

I was falling and falling. I tumbled down until striking the ground, raising a mist of hot, powdery sand. As the winds died and the clouds of sand settled, orange and brown rock formations appeared within the dune covered horizon. Beneath me the sand sparkled and throbbed with the intense heat rising from it.

My side ached from where I'd fallen. I limped toward the massive stone formations, seeking a shady nook to escape the oppressive heat. As I neared, I noticed a small group of people, each wrapped from head to toe in blue and turquoise fabrics. They were huddled beneath the shade. They looked up as I approached. Stared motionlessly. Eyes wide. Jaws hanging open. They looked at me as though I'd just fallen from the sky. They waited for me to speak. And when I did I told them all about my dog.

My Roommate's Girlfriend

My roommate Lawrence had an imaginary girlfriend. I'd invite him to a party or some movies and he'd say, "I can't. I've got to go meet Lenka." Sometimes we have friends here, visiting from the US. They're often curious about our love lives, wanting to know some good gossip. So Lawrence would tell them about Lenka.

"I didn't ask her out while she was my student," was how he usually began. "I waited until after she left school," he'd say.

"She was interested in seeing exhibitions, so we started going to openings. She was really kind of nervous about being with me. She hadn't had so many boyfriends. Actually – not that I'm bragging or anything – she was still a virgin. So I was her first real experience."

I heard him once talking on the phone to his parents back in the States. "We haven't been going out all that long. And I'm not sure I want to be in a serious relationship right now. We'll see what happens."

I don't know what he actually did when he went out with Lenka. Maybe he just sat in some neighborhood worker's pub, drank beer, and practiced his Czech with the locals. At that time, he tended to avoid the city center and any place where foreigners and tourists congregated. On one occasion, my friend Margo saw him standing alone in line outside Aero Kino.

"I'm here with Lenka," he told her. "She just went to the toilet for a second."

Margo invited him for drinks after the movie.

"Sorry, can't. Lenka's taking me to a party. It's her friend Hanna's *name day*. Some other time."

I somewhat understood Lawrence's behavior – odd as it was. There's something about having a girlfriend that makes everyone think you're normal. If you're not seeing someone, people assume you're damaged goods. There's this Catch-22 in which no one wants to date you if you're available, only if you're already in a relationship – in which case you're not available. So, by having an imaginary girlfriend, Lawrence makes himself far more desirable to other women, while only having a somewhat imaginary commitment to the girl he's imaginarily dating.

What freaks me out, though, is when he'd bring Lenka home at night. I'd be lying in bed, just about to nod off, when I'd hear his key scraping against the door, trying to find the keyhole. Then the knob wiggling, the door squeaking open and Lawrence making a loud *SHHHHHHHHHHHH!*

He'd whisper something like, "Try not to make too much noise. I think Ken's asleep." He'd remove his shoes, maybe drop them on the floor a couple of times to make it sound like two pairs, then tip toe into his room.

That's when I'd try like hell to fall quickly asleep. I didn't like to hear the bed squeaks from the other side of the wall and my roommate's heavy breathing and quiet gasps of "Lenka! Lenka! Oh, God. Lenka!"

How many months did this go on for? It seemed like an entire year, though it was probably only a couple months. After that, Lawrence met Valerie, an American girl studying film at FAMU. Valerie wasn't quite the Czech hottie Lawrence had dreamt of, but she was cute, intelligent, and probably had more in common with him than Lenka ever did.

I tried to make Lawrence feel guilty about dumping Lenka so suddenly, but he was untroubled by it.

"Lenka's young. She'll get over it," he said. "She probably had other guys waiting in the wings before we even split up."

"Lenka? Little, sweet Lenka? That doesn't sound like the girl you described to me."

"Oh, c'mon. All Czech girls are like that," Lawrence said, with a dismissive wave of his stale bread roll.

I wouldn't know. I'd never dated a Czech girl. In fact, I hadn't been dating all that much. I found myself somewhat caught in the non-dating Catch-22 of availability.

I wasn't desperate to solve the problem though. I had a heavy workload. I poured all my energy into proofing English translations of Czech pharmaceutical manuals, business directories and product safety instructions.

Yet...

Seeing Lawrence arm in arm with Valerie at Alan's Thanksgiving party made me think I should, perhaps, make some changes in my life, enjoy more free time. Maybe share the holidays with someone special.

That very evening, after Lawrence left the party to spend the night at Valerie's, I searched through his room. In his top dresser drawer I found a sheet of paper with a list of names. Right below Jim Freeman's number was written *Lenka,* a heart drawn next to it and a phone number.

That's how it began.

Lenka, it turns out, did not have any other boyfriends waiting in the wings. She had been just waiting there. Waiting for me actually.

Though she had never met me, never knew I even existed, something at the core of her being told her that all her life she had been waiting for someone like me. I promised I would never use her the way Lawrence had, that I would not dump her for the first real woman who came my way. I promised that things would be different between her and me. I am not one to cast stones. Her past doesn't matter to me. Not one bit. After all, it's not her fault she's imaginary.

Taking Care of Montreal

I wake up and – it's happening again – she's there beside me, *my wife!* How can this be? What became of Melissa, the office temp, the perky, pleated-skirt blonde B.U. MBA student? How did my wife find me, once again, spending the night in a cheap South Boston hotel on a night I said I'd be out of town?

She wakes. Her head turns a bit, revealing an amorphous drool mark on her pillow. Her steel gray eyes ease open and rest upon me. She smiles. She must be enjoying this trick of hers. She rolls to her side. I spot the mole over her left areola and the sharp lines of her collar bone, inky details of her body that have been indelibly set in my mind over six and a half years of marriage.

She moistens her lips. She says, "Good morning."

It is unmistakably her voice, throaty and strained, a bit coarse from years of cigarette smoke – though, unlike myself, she quit cold turkey two years ago March and hasn't had one since.

I can't speak. She is looking at me as if awaiting a reply to a question. She wants me to be surprised again. She wants me to stammer and say, "But – but – you?! How? What – where is..."

But I can't say anything. My tongue is a cactus

leaf. My gums dry as sand.

She rolls onto her back, her breasts lay flat. She is thirty-eight, same age as myself, but still has the figure of someone in her early twenties. She sighs, staring at the exposed light bulb hanging from the ceiling.

I think hard over the details of what has happened. Maybe I missed something. Or maybe something I thought happened last night was just something I dreamt. Did I dream Melissa? Did I dream those lies I told my wife, dream the phone call from my car phone saying I was on my way to the airport to take care of a company emergency in Montreal? Did I dream taking Melissa to dinner at Fitzroy's and ordering her her first martini ever? Did I dream the sex? God, tell me I didn't dream that. At least let that part be real, because it's almost as if I can still feel it, still feel the contradictory weightiness and buoyancy of it in my head and body.

She lets out a little moan. She seems very pleased with herself.

This is the third time she has done this to me. Every time it is with a different girl at a different hotel. I don't know what she does with them. I don't ask. I avoid speaking with these girls ever again. Never return their calls. Lenora, a sales rep from the Chicago office, I've seen twice since our tryst in a Plymouth motor lodge. She treats me rather coldly, but I don't have the guts to ask how she and my wife managed to switch places in the middle of the night without my noticing.

You have to question what it all means, I tell myself. A plot. A conspiracy. Some not-so-subtle subterfuge concocted by my wife to humiliate me. And these girls – are they not in complicity, luring me into this fraudulent infidelity designed to make me question my own sanity?

But I just don't know where my wife would have met Lenora. And there's absolutely no way she could have known Claudia, the French tourist, who was only in Boston for six days. Claudia spoke very little English and my wife knows no more French than what's written on the menus of certain restaurants in town.

"I'm hungry," she says, still looking up at the ceiling. "I'm ravenous."

She turns and draws close to me. Her scent. It *is* her. She reaches below the sheets and touches me. She wants to make love again.

I pull away. No. I tell her, *No*. I tell her she must stop doing this. I say, "Don't you see? This is wrong. Be angry with me. That's an understandable reaction. But don't keep doing this and pretending like nothing has happened."

She feigns a puzzled look.

"Goddamn you!" I shout. I sit up. I raise my palms and close my eyes. I'm trying to remain clam. Trying to.

"Please," I tell her. "Just leave."

This time she gathers her clothes without a word.

I will get dressed. I will have a cigarette, eat breakfast down the street, and get to the office before eleven. This evening when I arrive home she will try to pretend again like nothing has happened. She may even say, "Did you take care of Montreal? They must have snow by now. Was it cold?" This time, though, I may not be able to go along with the pretense.

This time I may have to put an end to it for good.

Lightning Strikes Again

She, Janis, likes to eat. Likes to cook, likes to eat. Adores food as her salvation. Her prophet is a veal cutlet, her Virgin Mary a dungeness crab leg drenched in lemon and butter. Her God… am I not her God, her true redeemer? Would any other man lay down his life for her as I would? I would walk naked in a lightning storm across an eighteen-hole golf course carrying an aluminum sign post for her – that is, if I thought it would do her any good (I am a pedagogical and effectuating deity). Maybe it would. She is in desperate need of absurd acts of salvation, absurd acts designed to free her of that death burden of "Do the Right Thing." There is a Catholic nun with a wooden ruler inside that pert-nippled bathing beauty body. She is oppressed by her moral outrages. She is oppressed into staring at the wall, into biting her nails, into cleaning then re-cleaning the apartment before dust can ever get a foothold. (Cleanliness isn't really next to godliness; it's only a way of telling the devil, "Don't bother me, I'm busy.")

She wants to make me her lover, but she is married. It's complicated. Her husband is a pilot. He flies a San Francisco to United Arab Emirates route and spends most of his time living in hotels. They have not shared the same bed in almost two years. He is uncertain he wants a divorce because of the child.

The child is almost three and lives with Janis's mother in Daly City. Janis and her husband cannot agree on the correct terminology for their relationship, whether they are *estranged*, *separated* or *through*.

I have taken Janis to the top of Mount Tam for a picnic, to sit and watch the sun set over the lovely city of San Francisco on a warm autumn evening. She is nervous, a bit upset, unsettled by the stillness in the air and the dark clouds moving slowly south along the Pacific Coast. She is worried for *me*. She thinks there is something supernormal about my body, some highly synergistic alignment of mineral energies, because I have, during the course of my brief thirty-four years on earth, been struck twice by lightning.

I haven't yet made up my mind whether they (the lightning strikes) were just complete coincidence or not. My metaphysical beliefs have been in disarray ever since age seventeen when Rabbi Roth lent me Spinoza's *Ethics* to read. It seems to me that saying, in effect, the rules of logic *are* God is an insult to both logic and God. Science, for example, doesn't seek to create mystery or to transcend logic. And an infinite God, I don't imagine, would create a world without mystery, that is, a world that adheres solely to the limited confines of man's logic.

But I am not all that sure of this. I sometimes think of the first lightning strike as a message from the heavens, instructing my body what to believe, and that I was too dense to understand, or too shocked by the lack of subtlety in the message for it to truly register upon the overcharged hormonal impulses of my pubescent physiognomy. The second strike was then perhaps thrown at me in anger and irritation that the first strike taught me nothing.

I sometimes imagine God to be like a frustrated vaudevillian during the early years of film. The routines that proved so effective for Him in the past – your floods, plagues, burning bushes, disembodied voices, solar eclipse, fire from the sky – these tricks no longer hold an audience's attention very long. He must now compete with the big screen stars of science and technology. And science is only too eager to paint the vaudeville antics of religion as low-brow entertainment. It thumbs its nose at church, temple, and mosque while cruising past in sleek convertibles, up and down the super highway of an expanding universe.

But science, too, has its questionable bag of tricks and rests ultimately on the precarious foundation of one simple question, the one repeatedly asked by each and every three-year-old of middling intelligence that has ever existed, *But why?*

I am not pious. I'm too immersed in the physicality of being, in the mystery of *what is,* to be overly concerned with *why is it?*

I'm thinking about all this now only because of Janis who is considering, on this eve, to make me her lover, but is afraid of – if not divine retribution or bad karma – skewing the moral balance of her life. She believes she is a good person. Unlike me, she places the *why?* before the *why not?* I believe she could be a better person if she weren't so damn good.

She says, "I am not like you, Harold. I can't balance moral complexities. I can't take two conflicting ideas and make them harmonize."

I say she is wrong, that that's exactly what we each do every day. Life is defined by conflict and synthesis.

She says, "Do you want that last chicken thigh?"

"No, you have it."

"Please."

She pulls the thigh out of the container and puts it on my plate. She wants the thigh, really, but she is giving it to me. This is what I mean. Giving me the thigh is not synthesis, it is not truly living, it is being *good*, but avoiding our ultimate duty, which is *to be*, to be who we are and to be present in this world. I don't really want the thigh, but I eat it anyway to teach her this lesson.

The rain holds off until the sun has completely vanished into the Pacific, the frayed party streamers of orange, pink and yellow cirrus clouds now dissolving into the deepening blues of twilight.

We are set upon by dark angry nimbus clouds from the north that don't have time or patience for childish sunsets. These are the alchemical clouds sent here to restore balance to some fucked-up renegade ions in the atmosphere. These are clouds with holsters packing white heat and explosives. They've come to reestablish law and order in the Bay Area and don't much care who or what gets hurt in the process. These are American clouds, pragmatic and heavy footed.

Janis says, rising on her knees, "Let's get going now. Okay? It's going to start pouring any second."

"Let me finish this thigh first."

"You like to tempt fate, don't you?"

She says that, not with anger or disapproval, but with a certain respect (reverence?). I am a mystery to her. She would not be interested in me if I were so easy to figure out. If I were easy to figure out she would know in which column of her moral ledger to place me and then, when all is balanced, I would cease to exist for her.

Somewhere near Stinson Beach a bolt of lightning shoots down. Ions have recanted their waywardness and are brought back in line. Still, more must be brought back into the fold. Black clouds prowl on, eyeing the rolling hills of redwoods and the cliffs of Mount Tam.

A drop of rain lands upon my upper lip. Then another on my forehead. Janis is sealing the half empty food containers. She gets up and places them in the trunk of my old BMW parked nearby. I throw the chicken bones into a nearby bush and begin folding up the blanket.

Janis gets into the passenger seat and holds the door open. "Hurry up there. It's really coming down."

I am almost in a mind to resist, to stand my ground defiantly, not be run off by a little water and the bellicose threats of expanding warm gases. But I fear Janis may misinterpret this as a suicidal death wish and I wouldn't know how to adequately explain to her that it is, in fact, quite the opposite.

Melissa's Creations

No one makes mud like Melissa. No one pours with such specificity the water needed for perfect mud, nor stirs so evenly the congealing crud of dirt and leaves. There is no one but me who quite understands.

She is a fixture in our playground. I see her working at it every day, perfecting her craft – and then some – until it is not craft alone, but perhaps a ritual or incantation. Mud comes alive within her small open palms. She works it into patties that appear light as air. She pulls it like taffy till there forms a squat bearded man, an archipelago, or the beating heart of a dragon. I've seen small animals come alive as fingers sculpt their form, poke holes for eyes, pry open tiny mouths. I've seen them squirm out of her grip, slip across the playground, and disappear beneath the metal chain-link fence.

Every day I worship Melissa from a distance. Every day I kneel and pray as she places her pink pail to the fountain's mouth. I bow low in supplication as a thin sacramental stream pours atop her sandy creations. She waves branches like wands, stirring the air before churning the mud. And in me I feel a peculiar burning, something flowing through me like warm blood. Heat rises through the ash and clay, the muck and sand from which I'm made.

Grubs and roots, they pulse like veins. I breathe deep the air and kiss the ground her hands have pulled me from.

The Book Group

A member of the Book Group came into the store the other day. She asked me to order twelve copies of Grisham Allende's *House of Dispirits*. I suggested, if they were interested in Latin American Magical Realism, they might try Jorge Luis Borges, Gabriel García Márquez, Julio Cortázar or Carlos Fuentes, maybe, but Allende was incredibly over-rated.

The woman pierced her brows together, curled up the left side of her lip and snarled, "Listen, unless you want me to start cracking a few spines around here you better order those Allende books and keep your trap shut."

They were like that, those Book Group members. Sometimes they came into the store, a few of them, and I'd see them roughing up some of the regular customers with their recommendations to buy shit like *The Alchemist's Daughter's Secret Diary*, *The Peculiar Sadness of Grass, The Girl Who Killed Corduroy, The Potato Diaries, The Cellophane Properties,* or *The Blind Potter's Recipe Guide to Divorce*. You couldn't ask them to leave or say anything without them starting a scene.

A previous store manager once confronted a couple Book Group members who kept trying to place copies of *The Bridge Club of Mattawan County* in the front window display. She asked them politely to stop twice before telling them to leave the store. They left without a fuss, but waited outside in the parking lot. When the manager left work, they grabbed her, forced her into their Toyota Corolla and made her listen to an audio recording of Elizabeth Tan reading from her book *Bone Joy, Luck Pray* over and over again for several hours.

Many times we filed police reports. But the police didn't care. One of the police captains, it seems, is also a Book Group member.

They got away with all kinds of shit – implausible murder mysteries, soporific story lines, cheap plot devices, wooden prose, kitschy sentimentality, linear narration – you name it. They inflicted their tastes not only on their own members, but on just about every book lover in town.

A close friend of mine was reading *Finnegan's Wake* at the Bagel Nook when a Book Group member cornered him, pulled the book from his hands and replaced it with a copy of *The Piano Thief's Widowed Nanny*.

As the Book Group member turned to leave the café, my friend worked up the nerve to ask, "What's wrong with what I was reading?"

The Book Group member stopped at the doorway, turned toward my friend and glared. "To answer that, I would have to read this pretentious crap and I'd eat my iPad before that."

He spat on the cover of *Finnegan's Wake*, shoved it through the flapping THANK YOU panel of the trash disposal and left the café.

Everyone knew Book Group members were tough. They had to be to get through such things as *Daughter of Misfortune, A Year According to Macaroons, Like Waterford Chocolate, The Mermaid's Hidden Notebook, The Honey Maker's*

Bee Garden, The Sassy Sister's Wooden Leg and *The Time Changer's Waif*. But no one was certain just how far they were willing to push things.

Rumor had it they once took on a Nora Bradford Steel historical whodunnit; a biography, *Bo Obama: My Tail to Tell* and a collection of paranormal romance fiction by the singer Jimmy Buffett. I tend to think those rumors were exaggerated and that the Book Group's tastes were not nearly so lethal.

My fellow employees at the bookstore and I got together one lunch break to discuss what to do about the Book Group. We took our sack lunches to the park and sat on benches beneath the water-gurgling fountain of three languid sirens.

Naomi, peeling the cellophane from her Dolphin safe tuna and whole grain sandwich, suggested we try subverting their tastes.

"How do you propose we do that?" Ryan asked.

"Infiltrate their ranks. Propose alternative selections. Point them in a new direction."

I laughed, remembering that was Sybilla's plan five years ago. This was before any of them started working at the bookstore.

"Who's Sybilla?"

"What happened?"

I took a swallow of lukewarm filter coffee and tried to explain how Sybilla joined the Book Group in order to change them. Instead, she turned into a diehard Book Group junkie. She became aesthetically disorientated, losing all sense of discernment, reading everything they placed into her hands. It was sad to see. She was eventually fired from the bookstore for doubling up orders on *Memos of a Shiksa*.

We sat in silence, glumly masticating our victuals to the rhythm of the water dribbling nymphs behind us. The Book Group seemed as undefeatable as they were indefatigable in their mission to dominate the cultural milieu of our town.

The sick thing is, though, that as much as they terrorize us, the bookstore probably wouldn't be in business without them. They are like mites in our fur, making us scratch with discomfort, while gnawing away at the bacteria that threaten to overcome us. The Book Group may never preen away the excess William H. Gass, Robert Coover or John Barth that accumulates like dust at the top of each bookcase, but the sense of fear the Book Group instills in each and every one of us forces us to hold dear what books we value most, lest they should be born upon a wave of literary success and their great allure drown beneath the undertow of sudden popularity.

The Hostage

I always fall in love with my captors. Like the time I was loaded into the blue and white Aerostar, blindfolded and whisked out of Lima, high into the Peruvian mountains, into the great yawning vault of Incan history and was told to keep my *cabasa* and my *asno hermoso* down as we hit potholes that made the van's chassis scrape against dirt and gravel. All the time the hard clean air of the Cordillera Blanca shale, granite and flowering cacti flooded through the van's open windows, mixing with the sweet and meaty scent of my captor's cigar smoke.

They took me to a camp of dilapidated buildings with walls of adobe brick and rooftops of corrugated metal held down by large rocks. I slept on a dirt floor, wrapped in beautifully woven turquoise and chocolate brown alpaca blankets. Someone always waited outside my door in case I tried to escape. But there was nowhere to escape, really.

They fed me mainly avocados, cactus fruit and soups of stewed meats, onions and potatoes. But on my birthday, they served me the peppery-spiced heart of a yak.

When I grew bored of playing the hapless prisoner, I helped around the camp with cooking and washing. Evenings, I sat with them by the fire, drank excellent Peruvian red wines and learned their songs in Spanish and Quechua.

In our fields grow the spines
That pierce the boots of tyrants
While Quechua are enchained
I carry with me a big gun
And something to cuddle with at night

Or something like that. I'm translating, of course.

At the time my husband's lawyers made the payoff – leaving 10,000 US dollars in a sewer pipe along the Javier Prado, a sort of red light district in Lima – I was three streets away, blindfold lifting from my eyes, and my blood teeming with anxiety and sorrow over having to leave the Aerostar and the mountain life I had grown to love.

"*Buena suerte*," said Chico, as he slid open the van door. His semi-toothless mouth smiled wide. Using a few words of English I had taught him, he added, "*Fight da powe', mi amiga!*"

From his driver seat, Nicanor turned and winked. "*Adiós mi pequeña enjauladita*."

I didn't want to step out of the van. I wanted to say, "Let those *Americanos* keep their filthy dollars. We have something nobler: purpose, fortitude, *una causa*."

I knew, however, from past experiences that things change once you give up the status of being hostage and become a willing captive. It is never the same again. The fear and uncertainty that intensifies life and emotions turns to boredom, depravation and routine.

...As it did in Macau with the Cantonese mafia who kept my arms and legs bound in silk braces for twenty-nine extraordinary days. After the hostage money was delivered, I convinced them to let me stay on in their penthouse apartment with its extravagant bonsai roof garden. But having chosen to stay, everything seemed to change. I was free to come and go as I pleased. The men no longer worried about me and often went about their business as if I wasn't there.

I fell into a routine of morning gardening, afternoons watching Korean soap operas dubbed into Cantonese, and evenings watching bootleg videos or playing high-stakes *mah jong*, while chain smoking *Mann Si Fat* cigarettes.

Baltazar held out his palm. His long, meticulously filed nails looked like small white spades. "Lemme see your tiles, *Bu Duan Bin*." *Bu Duan Bin*, being what he called me, meaning something like *Constant Guest*.

"I'm fine. I think I can do this by myself."

He shrugged. His pinstriped shoulder pads rose up and down like pneumatic levers.

Truthfully, I had little idea what I was doing. I knew that "suit" tiles were numbered and "honor" tiles were without numbers and in Chinese characters I couldn't read. And that flowers were bonus tiles to be discarded right away – something I often forgot to do. Mostly I tended to just arrange tiles in pleasing patterns and hope to get a *chow* or a *pung*.

"You no hold *flowas*, now?"

"Christ, Baltazar. You never give me a break. Just let me make my own mistakes."

"You es fwee to do what you want, *Bu Duan Bin*."

"Okay. Fine. I quit."

Days passed. I continued to learn from Old Hasai, the gardener, how to wire and knot the dwarfish trunks and limbs of bonsai trees, so they persisted in twisting and curling like frozen plumes of smoke. But my interest in them began to wane along with my increased freedom.

One morning I awoke before all the others, dressed into my American slacks and blouse, and left the building, never to return.

I still look back at that seaside captivity, however, with a sort of heartache. And longing.

But lives move on.

As mine did from captor to captor. Even in Laos, where I was taken hostage by the Liberation Army along the road from Luang Prabang to Vientiane, and was underfed, cold and treated with contempt for most of my confinement – even there I felt a certain – shall I say "escape?" – within my forced captivity.

Yes, for even the worst of these moments I still yearned once released and returned to the US, my husband, my home and my comfortable life in suburban Pennsylvania.

Ensconced in my pillowed window seat amidst trellised ivy, spider ferns, lace curtains and enmeshed morning shadows, I read the international pages of The New York Times and The Washington Post.

Tamil Tigers in Sri Lanka. Russian Mafia in Ukraine. Costa Nostra in Sicily. Moro Islamic Liberation Front. Bogotá Cocaine Cartels. Chechen Freedom Fighters. Basque Separatists. Taliban Militia. Karen Rebels. Afghani War Lords. Columbian FARC. God's Army. Hezbollah. Khmer Rouge. Montoneros. M-19's. Red Army. Janjaweed. Lord's Resistance. Shining Path...

Reading their litany of names in the headlines causes my imagination to soar and my heart to beat like the wings of a nectar-crazed hummingbird.

As I envision the multiple possibilities of captivity, I can almost feel my Pennsylvanian roots crowding beneath me. Choking on depleted terrain. Constricted within their cage of fealty. And aching for a way out once more.

Anima Husbandry

She took apart her husband. Unhinged the knees, unsnapped the clasps at each hip, rotated the head counterclockwise until it loosened enough to pull free, then set about with custom wrenches, painstakingly disjoining each section, removing piece by piece and placing them each within their assigned, contour foam rubber compartments inside the large metal carrying case.

It took nearly three hours to get her husband completely unassembled and packed away. She wasn't looking forward to the job of reassembly and thought to herself that whoever invents a husband that can be taken apart or put back together in less than fifteen minutes is going to make a killing.

She was taking him to Paris. She had always dreamed of living in Paris, the city of virtual appetites and gastronomic mainframes. She had all sorts of crazy notions about life in Paris. Mostly related to the old Paris, the Paris of the early 21st century when Parisians had given up speaking French and making films and learned to enjoy American culture and English language.

Those had been heady times. The era of the Young Moldavians. They flooded the city, able to afford living stylishly in Paris due to the immense strength of the rufiyaa. Some of the greatest contemporary works in English language were written by twenty-something Moldivian expats. Most of the really great holographic motion sculptures, subatomic *happenings*, and plasma canvases were also created by young Moldavians living the bohemian life in Paris at that time.

But Paris had changed.

People no longer spent much time in the hot, arid streets. Life moved into environmental domes and inhabitable theaters, great amusement parks of images and sound where people spent their entire days.

Subsequent generations of Moldavians, Timorees, Inuits and the youths of other affluent nations began setting up expatriate communities elsewhere, like Vladivastock, Calgary and, for a short time, the Prince Joseph Islands (before the tragic bioengineering disaster that released hundreds of thousands of carnivorous moths).

Her husband didn't want to go to Paris. He knew life there was harsh for husbands. Spare parts were overpriced and difficult to find. Husbands in Paris were mostly K-12 Graduates, a popular model manufactured by Hasbro. Very affordable, but fairly unreliable. He was Princeton GP-800, Fabio edition, with souped-up Tickler and Black Mambo components. If anything went wrong, he might lay idle for weeks on end waiting for a shipment of replacement parts.

Then again, how bad could that be? Might give his battery a chance to fully recharge.

He had heard of a time when husbands were flesh born. This was back when DI's (*designed identities*) were still called artificial intelligence or, among the vulgar classes, "robots." Though such machines were still far too primitive to be suitable husbands.

Among their many drawbacks, flesh born husbands stayed with their wives, on average, a mere seven years – with the exception of some lunar colonies where husbands changed wives every seventy-two hours. The development of iMates and DI husbandry changed all that.

Some people still lament the rapid decline and near extinction of flesh born husbands and the days when, as they used to say, it was a man's world and men ruled the roost, wore the pants in the family, brought home the bacon and inseminated organically. But, most would agree, those were views born purely out of nostalgia and served little practical purpose.

As the lid came down upon his head – latches clicking in place; tumblers turning, scrambling the lock's combination – her husband thought, as all husbands are programmed to think, "Yes, I am very lucky to have been made in these times."

What a War!

We were all going to the war. It was certain to be an historic event and years from now we would look back and say, Yeah, we were there. It kicked ass.

I was lucky to have gotten into the war. Most of those going had signed up long before the war was ever declared. Those, like me, who decided to go at the last minute, had to hustle to get enlisted in time. Steve Gardner, who went with me to sign up, was turned away because he was a methadone addict and had needle marks up and down his arms. Jerry Sesnowsky, got turned back because of the gay pride flag tattooed on his left calf. Shauna Westmueller was a butch dike, but kept quiet about it and they let her in. Fortunately, things were so chaotic around the recruiting office I was never asked about my criminal record. I was passed through, got my papers and, before you knew it, I was on my way to West Virginia to get my basics done and shipped off to the war!

It turned out to be an amazing war. Despite having signed up last minute, I was able to get up close to the action and really see everything going on. The lights! Incredible. The ground vibrating beneath my feet. Smoke rising up in columns. The scent of chemical fires and burning flesh clinging to the blackened insides of my nostrils. Everyone – I mean *everyone* – screaming their heads off. It was completely insane.

Amazing pyrotechnics. All performed with precision timing. If you've ever seen any film footage, you sort of know what I'm talking about.

I felt a little sad that my girlfriend, Lorie, wasn't there to see it. She had wanted to come, but couldn't get off work. It was lousy timing. But, whatever. There were plenty of other hot babes who were totally into war, and they knew far more about war than I did. It's like they'd been following wars all of their lives, while I had only recently started getting into them.

During breaks from the action, I hung out with some of these girls in the rec. hall, drinking Cokes and playing ping pong. I even messed around a little with one of them, Angie, this really cute private from Des Moines.

Angie was really big on war. Her grandfather had been a twenty star general or some shit like that. She knew about practically every war there was and who was there and what kind of ammo they used and who scored the biggest hits where. Like a real encyclopedia of war.

She asked what I thought of the war.

"Pretty cool," I said.

"Yah, for sure," she said.

In the muddy, unlit alley between the rec. and the mess tents, I grabbed hold of Angie. She let me kiss her. Only for a moment. Then she got weird on me.

"I don't know if this is a good idea," she said.

"It's okay. We're both privates."

I knew I wasn't going to get very far with Angie, though. After a bit, I ditched her outside the telecommunications trailer by pretending to go get us some Cokes.

I got back out to the war just when things had slowed down some. Most of the lights flashing were from people lighting up cigarettes or sending text messages. I weaved quickly through the crowd of swaying bodies. Then a big blast knocked me off my feet. Wow! Damn! Shit! I quickly got back up and started running faster and faster toward the large flames in the distance. I wanted to get up close to those flames. I wanted to feel their furnace heat prickle against my skin.

Someone stuck out an arm trying to stop me, maybe wanting to see a pass to go further, but I shoved my way through and kept running until I felt dizzy and my legs were really heavy like sandbags. Then I just fell to my knees in the dirt.

As I dropped, I felt something shove into my side, like a half broken china plate. I placed a hand there and it felt all soggy   the shirt and whatever was coming out of it. I couldn't see. I held my hand in front of my eyes. I could barely trace the outline of my fingers.

At that moment, I knew I wasn't just watching the war. I was a part of it and it was a part of me and I would follow the war, go on tour wherever it went, for as long as I could. But not just then. Just then I was really tired. I laid down in the dirt. I fell asleep there – a really, really deep sleep – and the rest of the war – the rest of my life, really – is all a blank to me now.

The Replacement

It was all coming together. There was a palpable exhilaration in the room after my presentation concluded. I'd truly opened the eyes of upper management to the dramatic improvements rail and waterway distribution through inland cities such as Jiangxi held over the relatively expensive and over capacity port cities like Shanghai and Tianjin, assuredly saving the company a minimum of 3.4 million over the next four years. Dale Evans whispered to me, as we walked triumphantly out of the boardroom, "Holy shit, man. You've been crackin' them numbers." And old man Michaelson blinked his furry white brows and said, "Very impressive stuff, Paul."

I owe it all to my new knee. Ever since my knee transplant my life has improved radically. Not only am I walking without joint pain, but I've noticed improvements in bicycling, lifting heavy objects, meditation, piano playing, number crunching…

What a difference in concentration it makes not having to worry about knee pain any more! And my potential seems unbounded. Why not take up rock climbing, kick boxing, run for local office, learn Mandarin, start my own consulting firm, start dating again?

It was different before the surgery. My knee was

on its last legs, so to speak. They moved ahead my operation date after I'd really messed things up at the Starlight Cabaret Halloween party. I had gone dressed as a mummy, gauze-wrapped as if I'd broken every bone in my body. Ha. Ha.

Sheila Arnold was out on the dance floor, one of my colleagues from work, an ambitious young account administrator who'd recently graduated from Oberline. She was beautiful and bright as hell. But she barely acknowledged my presence. I'd see her rushing around the fourteenth floor and call out some jovial quip like "Where's the fire?" and she'd turn and leer at me as if I'd said, "Nice ass."

At the Monster Ball, she was dressed in a short white tennis dress with a gold belt and a *fleur de lys* sewn into the front. She wore gold, knee-high boots and carried a wooden sword. She-Ra: Princess of Power. I recognized the outfit immediately from my Indiana University days watching He Man cartoons while drinking Pabst Blue Ribbon and smoking reefer most afternoons. She was bobbing her tiara-adorned head and long blonde hair to the shaggy beat of The Cure's "Jumping Someone Else's Train." I tried to move closer and, in doing so, tripped over my bandages. It was as if an invisible hand had yanked me down.

My bad leg twisted beneath me. I heard someone laugh. Almost immediately I passed out.

I was off work for three weeks. This was at a time when the company was making serious managerial changes and corporate restructuring moves. It was not entirely clear I would have a job to go back to once my new knee was in place.

But it didn't turn out that way. Before I knew it, I was walking fine and back on the job. My boss, Jerry Schwartz, immediately moved me to the Asian expansion team where I thrived on the intense deadline pressure.

Schwartz is a man of few words and fewer complements. When I passed him in the hall soon after my successful presentation, he raised his hand, high five'd me, and kept walking. That was as high a complement as anyone could expect from him, so I was feeling pretty good about job security. So much so, I got on the phone right then and made an appointment with a realtor to do some serious apartment shopping on the North Side. It was time to become a homeowner, not a renter. Time to move up in the world.

A moment after hanging up with the realtor, the phone beeped with a new caller. It was my ex-girlfriend Rhonda. We hadn't spoken in over a year, not since she left me for the dentist.

"I hope I'm not disturbing you at work," she said.

"No, that's okay. What's up?"

She said it was just a social call. She thought of me recently and wondered if I'd like to get dinner or lunch sometime.

When I asked about the dentist she said, "Oh. That's long over. He turned out to be a real nitrous oxide freak."

"Knock. Knock," said David Manning. He stood at the doorless entrance to my office. "Interested in getting some Indian grub for lunch?"

This was new, being asked to lunch by one of the Princeton boys. Life was much different now that I had a new knee, exactly as my anesthesiologist predicted.

"Just relax, Take deep breaths," said Dr. Franks, as he placed the transparent elephant mask over my mouth. "Breathe... There... That's good. You'll be a new man after this."

At least that's what I thought he said. Just before everything went blank.

The three Princeton boys walked into Samsara Indian Restaurant like they owned the place. The waiter smiled and nodded.

Peter Kolarik said, "Hello Mani" He patted the waiter's shoulder as he passed.

The back wall of the restaurant held a mural. Blue elephants. Purple mountains. A multi-limbed Indian god dancing with an enraptured princess. At a table beneath the mural, sat two girls from the office. One was Sheila Arnold.

The girls invited us to join them. Sheila scooted over and gestured for me to take the seat beside her.

"I haven't seen you in a while, Paul."

Paul. She actually remembered my name. Before I could respond, she said. "You look different."

"Really? Well, I..."

"You have a new haircut?"

"No, actually I have a new knee."

"Wow. Knee surgery. I bet that hurt."

"No, not at all. I had a great anesthesiologist. Dr. Franks. Knocked me right out. Didn't feel a thing."

Mani came to distribute menus and take our drink orders, diverting Sheila's attention for a moment. She set down the gold menu of embossed buffalo hide and returned her attention to me.

"Of course you had anesthesia during the surgery. But something like that must hurt like hell when you wake up."

She turned completely toward me. It was the first time she'd ever looked directly in my eyes within such proximity. Her eyes were an intense jade with large dilated pupils so deep and so black they could perfectly reflect the entire room. Her lips parted and her delicate trim brows tilted outward in sympathetic concern.

"Wake up?" I asked her.

"Yes, when you came to after the surgery. That's when it must have really hurt."

I didn't quite grasp what she was getting at. Or maybe I did and was not quite ready for it.

"Wake up?" I said again not sure if I was actually speaking the words out loud or only to myself.

"Yes, wake up."

"What do you mean, *Wake up*?"

"You know. *Wake up*."

"Wake?"

"Yes, wake."

"Really? Wake?"

"Yes. *Wake up*."

"But – why? Why wake from all this?"

Missing

I spent most of the night warming my hands on mugs of hot tea, while trying to write Amelia a letter, telling her how empty my life was without her and how, if she only came back, things would be different this time. In the morning, after a few restless hours of sleep, I sealed the envelope, stuck it in my jacket pocket and left for work.

I stopped at the corner of the main intersection near my home. Across the street, two people were in line at the bank machine. In front of the Vietnamese grocery, an old woman stood beside the potato bin holding a spud to her ear as if it were a mobile phone. Down the steps, along Stitneho Street, a man in a shiny, turquoise suit whistled Mozart's *Marriage of Figaro* as he locked the rusted security gate outside Pink Dolly's nightclub. Everything was the same as any other morning – only the corner postbox was missing.

No problem. It would get to Amelia a day later, but I could easily mail the letter from work. So I walked on toward my office just past the Flora metro station.

I didn't get to within a block of Chaslavská Street before I felt something was amiss. Ahead of me, where there should have been towering brown plaster and suet covered windows, was nothing but blue sky and a cat's cradle of wires and sleeping pigeons.

As I neared, it became clear my office building was no longer where it had been for the past eleven years. In its place was a chain link fence surrounding a disarray of old machinery and derelict electric transformers.

There was nothing to do on a day like today but go home and crawl back into bed. I returned to Chlumova Street, opened the front door to my building and went inside.

Was it really my building though? Somehow the entry seemed roomier, the ceiling higher. No, that wasn't it. The stairs and banister were missing. Gone. A quick look outside confirmed that this was the right building number – only it was no longer quite the same place I had left only an hour before.

I had no choice but to scale the side of the building in order to reach my fourth floor apartment. By hoisting myself onto window ledges and pulling and clawing my way with the assistance of stone cornices, telephone cables, bent drainpipes and neglected flag holders, I slowly made my way up the façade. It was hard, sweaty work, but I managed okay – though at one point I barely kept from falling when a large, rusty eye-hook broke off in my hand, cutting deep into my palm.

Once through my window, I collapsed into a heap on the floor. I rested there a moment, relieved to be enveloped again in the dark safety of my own apartment, surrounded by familiar furnishing and well worn parquet floors. Maybe I shouldn't have left that morning. But how was I to know the day would start so oddly?

I ran cold water in the bathroom sink and washed the blood from my palm. I wrapped several layers of toilet paper around my hand until the blood stopped seeping.

In the kitchen, I lit a stove burner and put the kettle on. Reaching over the refrigerator, I grasped at the vodka bottle. (I don't usually drink before noon, but today seemed like a good day to make an exception.) As I lifted the bottle, I could feel its emptiness. Not a drop inside. The same was true for the Fernet and the bottle of Jack Daniel's Amelia had given me at Christmas.

It was only then true panic set in. My limbs trembled like cartoon electric wires baring too much current. Veins at my temples throbbed, making my head ache and my vision slightly double. I felt faint and a bit nauseous. Shadows from beneath the bookcase and sofa began to deepen and spread outward like spilled ink.

I didn't want to be alone at that moment. I reached for the cordless phone on the kitchen table, like a drowning man flailing for an oar or foam vest to keep afloat. She had told me never to call again, but I figured surely Amelia would understand this was an emergency.

My index finger quivered as I pressed the buttons. I waited anxiously to hear her soft drowsy voice, a trembling yawn from those peppermint-glossed lips. I would tell her everything that happened – losing my office, risking my life trying to get back into my apartment, the horrible cut in my palm that was – even then – opening itself again, blood weighing into the loosely wrapped tissue and causing it to clump apart.

Her empathy would dissolve her bitterness. I'd tell her about the letter, how I realized she was right. I had taken too much for granted. I could see that now she was gone.

I waited with the phone to my ear. I heard no

ringing, only the vague whisper of electric currents. I dialed again, more slowly. Then again. And again. I dialed her number over and over. Kept doing it, not believing she wasn't really still there.

We Celebrities

One day everyone became famous. Suddenly, the entire planet rose from obscurity, from the left handed bass player of a Rhode Island heavy metal trio who bussed tables by day to the Tibetan commode cleaner in a budget hotel ten kilometers southeast of Beijing. Everyone became known by all. Or nearly all. They had admirers. They had fans. Their pictures were taped on the insides of gym lockers or framed and hung on office cubicle partitions for inspiration. Everyone did this. I did this. And everyone knew their admiration was reciprocated in one form or another, by one person or another. They knew their image was being placed, poster size, upon hundreds of bedroom walls; licked and adhered to thousands of letters and postcards; detailed upon the hoods of automobiles and the side doors of vans. It was a mad frenzy of fame that swept the entire globe, crossing cultural barriers and national borders.

For a while, I was quite in awe of Inga, a German waitress from the Black Forest region. I wrote her fan letters. *Dear Inga, If only I were a stein in your hands!* I downloaded pictures of Inga from the Internet. Inga at work. Inga at play. Inga, coquettish, stepping out of the shower. Inga peeling potatoes in her kitchen sink. Inga repairing a flat on the vintage R23 BMW motorbike she, by herself, had completely restored. I was obsessed with Inga, but I was equally obsessed with Manuel, the eighteen-year-old Guatemalan boy who repaired and polished shoes on the streets of Guatemala City. Manuel was not the hardest worker, but he knew the lyrics to every U2 song ever recorded. I read all about Manuel in a fanzine devoted entirely to him.

There were dozens of others I was extremely devoted to at one time or another. Carlos, an Argentinean truck driver. Yo-Yo, a Japanese art student studying ceramics. Lek, a Thai travel agent. Ilsa, a Latvian policewoman. Those are the ones that first come to mind, but I can list dozens and dozens of others if you want, later. I don't mind. I can talk about each one for hours.

It's not known exactly why, suddenly, everyone became so famous. Some considered it an unexpected side benefit of the host-parasite and disease-vector relationship changes brought on by global warming. Some credited the democratizing force of the Internet and the increase in personal leisure. Those who'd already been famous thought it was a mass delusion, like UFO, Virgin Mary and Macaulay Culkin sightings. Academics and liberals considered it a spontaneous cultural rebellion against corporate manufactured celebrityhood. Some said simply that everyone just started to seem a lot more interesting, more interesting than they ever previously dreamed imaginable.

The Patch

Howard is a large, gray-bearded man, with a denim vest that bulges as much from his gut as from the numerous patches and emblems sewn on it, patches for Boy Scouting, auto racing, state parks, motor oil, movie studios, trade unions, state flags, assorted beer brands... even a peace sign, which is ironic given he is so keen on the war.

Howard is seated across from me at the new Vinohrady Mexican restaurant, pulling pork chunks off toothpicks and chewing as he speaks.

"I love it," he says, talking about the war. He grins somewhat defiantly. "It's damn exciting. Better than any movie. Explosions, violence, dead bodies... It'll be a damn shame when it's over."

He is baiting me. Am I supposed to say war isn't exciting? Am I supposed to bring up the obvious sadness and tragedies of war? I say nothing and let him go on.

"Now my goddamn CNN keeps cutting out," Howard fumes. "I don't know if it's the cable service or the TV."

The toothpick between his teeth shifts directions back and forth as he speaks.

"Maybe it's the TV. No one else seems to have the same problem. All the other stations come in fine. I don't know what the fuck it is."

He has been glued to CNN since the start of the war. He is only away from the TV this evening to attend this grand opening. He can part from the war for a couple hours for some free beer and skewered meat.

His wife – a pale, sturdy Czech woman, too young still for the bleach in her hair to cause any serious long-term damage – has made him promise not to speak about the war. She is seated at the other end of the table, just out of hearing distance. Howard, therefore, keeps clandestinely bringing up the subject, like he is sneaking hits off a cigarette.

After a couple long drags of diatribe, he exhales a sfumato of invectives and expletives, then cuts himself off saying, “I better stop now before she catches me,” only to resume the war talk after a few more moments.

“Don’t get me wrong,” Howard says, “I don’t think just any war is okay. I was around during Vietnam. I was living in San Francisco then. I protested that war. There was no reason for it. But this is different. 9-11 changed the world, changed the way I think about things. 9-11 is when things really hit home.”

He wipes a beer burp from his lip and says, “I’ve hated those goddamn ragheads ever since.”

“But 9-11 doesn’t have anything to do with Iraq,” I say, trying to anchor the conversation with the usual polemic being batted back and forth in opinion pages. “9-11 was caused by a group of Saudis. But we’re not attacking Saudi Arabia. They’re supposedly our friends.”

“Might as well kill the Saudis too,” Howard says. “And the Iranians and the Syrians. The whole lot of them. That part of the world is all just rot. Go there and tell me it isn’t. I have friends who’ve been there.

Those toilet-squatting assholes have turned the Middle East into one big cesspool."

Howard turns in his wife's direction. "Helena? Helena?"

She is in the middle of speaking to the Czech girlfriend of the Mexican restaurant's American owner. She raises a finger to tell Howard "one minute," while the owner's girlfriend finishes what she's saying. Then Helena turns to face Howard, saying, sweetly, "Yes?"

"Get me some of that dessert, would ya?"

Helena rises from her seat and obediently gets a slice of cake for Howard, just as she had done earlier for his second helping of nachos. She does it so obligingly, so like a nurse attending a patient, it makes me think Howard must have some sort of physical ailment that makes getting up and down incredibly difficult. I'd be surprised if there wasn't a walking stick or cane somewhere beneath the table.

"Thank you, Sweetie," he says, as his wife sets the cake before him.

"Well, it's a good time to be here," I say, meaning Prague, not necessarily the Mexican restaurant.

"She's the only thing good about being here," Howard says, indicating his wife. "Prague used to be nice, but it's all fucked up now."

"How long have you been here?" I say, a bit relieved we've turned the corner on all that war talk.

"Nine years. Left San Francisco in '94 and came here." He sighs. "I'd go back, but it's gotten too expensive. Couldn't even afford to breathe there now."

"So you're sort of in exile here."

"Let me tell you," Howard says, wiping white frosting off his gray mustache. "Life is one *long* fuckin' exile, man. Doesn't matter where you are. Doesn't matter if you're living in the same damn house you were born in. Every year is robbed from you. It slips behind the glass screen. Becomes memory. You can watch it over and over, but you can never be in it again."

He pulls a cigarette out of his Marlboro Light pack.

"Nothing good lasts," Howard says, smoke pouring out his mouth and nostrils. "There will never be a Utopian world. Once you accept that, things are easier. You enjoy what little you can get out of it."

"Is that the secret to life?" I ask, smiling as though it was a light, off-handed question. Actually, I mean it seriously.

"No," he says.

He looks down at the front of his vest, as if searching for a fallen piece of cake to snatch up with his fingertips. He points to a patch at about kidney level. It is a white skull and crossbones on a black rectangle, like the flag of a pirate ship. He shifts his weight as if about to rise and better show me, but aborts the effort and slumps back in his chair.

"Death," Howard says. "That's the secret to life. That's all you need to know."

Shelly's Café

"I saw him," Shelly told Frank over dinner at his place. She licked icing off her fingers as she explained. "He sat by the window and asked for a cappuccino with nutmeg." Frank found it difficult to that believe Mao Tse Tung was in Chicago. That Mao was still alive, yes, he could almost believe that, living a clandestine life in central Chile perhaps, deep in the jungle, writing his memoirs. But that he was in Chicago ordering cappuccinos and flipping through back issues of Northwestern Quarterly – that stretched his fertile imagination a bit too far. He was a playwright, but he was a realist too.

"Shelly," he said, wiping icing with his forefinger from the corner of her mouth. "Hon, don't drink so much coffee. It makes you anxious."

Shelly got that *fuck you* look in her eyes.

"It's not that I don't believe you," Frank quickly added. "It's quite possible it could have been Mao. Maybe not *quite* possible, but maybe, yes, something like that could have happened."

"Did."

"Okay, what if it did? What if that was Mao at your table? What does it mean? What does it matter? No one would care that Mao is alive and tipping poorly in Chicago. He's an anachronism, a relic of the past."

Trying to maintain a controlled sense of profundity, while pecking at a sofa button with her finger, Shelly said, "The past, Frank, is always in the present."

"The past is in the past," said Frank. "And the present is only a variation of the past, an alteration, but there is a separation."

Frank was speaking but no longer sure what he was saying. Words, he thought, perhaps as illusionary as Shelly's Mao, thoughts seated at the table of the mind calling out orders. Poor tippers them all!

Frank first met Shelly at a cast party. Not for a play he'd written or that she'd performed in, but one of those friend-of-a-friend-who's-generous-with-wine-and-deli-meats sort of affairs. She penetrated his personal space with Dijon breath and spilt Merlot on his Doc Martens.

"Brecht is my hero too," she said. "Emotions always fuck up the message. I don't want to be an emotional actress. I hate Stanislavsky. I want to be a vessel of truth. Is that a weird thing to say?"

Frank fingered the coins in his pocket, wondering if he had cab fare for two or if he would have to take her home to his place by bus.

"No," Frank said, "that's not such a weird thing."

A knock on the door woke Frank from a preparatory writing nap. He rose, opened the door and found Shelly, large-eyed, damp at the brow, a hand in her bag searching for the key he'd given her, the key he'd forgotten to ask for back that evening, weeks before, when he said they should start seeing other people.

"Frank, you're home."

"Where else am I supposed to be?"

She hurried past, threw her purse on the sofa and unbuttoned her shirt collar.

"I need a drink," she said. "Can I fix myself one?"

"I'll get it," Frank offered, walking toward the kitchen. "What do you want?"

"A gin something-or-other. No. Fuck that. A gin straight... No. Gin with ice. Squeeze in some lime... No. Just water."

"Gin and water?" Frank asked from the kitchen.

"No. Just water. I can't drink just yet. I have to keep my head straight."

Frank, glass in hand, emerged from the kitchen. Shelly gulped down the water before speaking.

"Goebbels," she said, placing the empty glass on the coffee table and pulling her bare feet up beneath her. "Goebbels," she said again, this time more vehemently. "The Nazi guy."

"I know who Goebbels is."

Frank rested a knee upon the sofa, leaning closer, listening patiently. She seemed angry he wasn't sharing her hysteria.

"He was at the café today. Sat at the same table as Mao."

"Mao came back today?"

"No!" She smacked the sofa with her palm, raising a puff of dust. "No, it was the same table where Mao sat before, but Goebbels was alone when he came. He ordered a decaf and sat there staring out the window until this guy comes in and I don't know who he is at first but when he sits with Goebbels and starts talking I recognize immediately it's James Cagney."

"How could you not recognize Cagney? All those films you've seen."

"This is different. It's not black and white. And he looks much older."

"I'd imagine so." Frank sat down and rested an arm over her shoulder.

"It's just so weird. Why are they going there?"

"I don't know," Frank said and felt stupid immediately for saying this. He thought he should either know why or know that what she was saying was untrue and explain why. He couldn't explain why. He loved her too much to impose upon her imagination, her sense of truth.

Her parents were control freaks. As a child, they kept her in group therapy and on fad diets. The only person she really trusted was her Uncle Irving. But he got locked up for some sort of indiscretion. In Joliet, visiting her uncle, little Shelly nearly started a riot tearing down the corridors shouting Uncle Irv is innocent, innocent, innocent! and everyone should be set free, free, free!

Perhaps Frank would have continued letting things go on this way, keeping notes in his journal about each new visitor that came to Shelly's café, but when Shelly began speaking with these visitors from the past, repeating very detailed conversations to him, he knew her problem had gotten serious. She had flown far from reality, her mind now nesting within the branches of illusion and escape.

"I'm learning so much," she told him one evening.

Frank was arranging decorative logs and branch sections within the artificial fireplace.

"Oscar Wilde said that appearances –"

"Wait. When did you see Oscar Wilde?"

"Last Wednesday. I told you this."

"No you didn't."

"Well, anyway. I saw him. He's very funny and not bad looking. He told me that appearances are reality and we shouldn't be fooled by those who say reality is something that runs underneath, something that needs excavating and interpretation."

"Wilde said that?"

"Yes. That's what I just told you. You're not a

good listener any more, Frank. I have to keep repeating things to you."

"It's just that I need to hear some of this stuff twice." Frank continued breaking branches into faux kindling as Shelly spoke on about Wilde.

He wondered if Shelly shouldn't be seeing a psychiatrist again. A director friend had given him a name, just in case, someone he said had treated nearly half the Chicago theatre community at one time or another.

"And today," Shelly continued, placing her bare feet upon the coffee table, "Raymond Chandler gave me another chess lesson. Before long I'll be beating even you."

A week passed and Frank was not yet able to bring up the subject of psychiatric help. And, what was worse, he had begun to feel the effects of her psychosis in himself. Involuntarily, his gruff Chicago realism was flowering into the fantastical. Characters underwent strange metamorphoses. People spoke with ghosts and had prophetic visions. He was writing work he knew would never be staged, work out of vogue with the Chicago theatre scene, but he had no control over what his imagination had begun to place upon paper.

He obsessed over Shelly's grasp of the unreal and it contaminated his thoughts like a rampant virus. He began to think curing Shelly was necessary for his own sake, for his writing to return to normal and perhaps for his own sanity.

Frank devised a plan. His director friend was organizing a party. He'd see to it the psychiatrist was there. Introduce him to Shelly. Get her to talk about her café visitors. This psychiatrist would certainly know how to coax Shelly in for treatment. It would be simple.

"The Forgetting of Being. That's what he called it."

Shelly was surrounded by a group, mostly men, all holding cocktails, some with cheese hors d'oeuvre and some with empty napkins.

"You're talking about Kant, right?" interrupted one young man, dark hair slicked straight back. Frank recognized him as the lead in *Goodnight, Dillinger,* which had recently opened at the Organic Theatre.

"She's talking about Heidegger," said the older man with a white goatee. He tucked his wire-rimmed glasses into the breast pocket of his green blazer. "Go on, Shelly."

"Yes, Shelly," another voice urged. "Finish your story."

"Well, Heidegger was all fidgety from drinking all those double espressos in a row. So when I began asking if maybe some people need specialized knowledge because it gives them order and stability to function within an amorphous world, and maybe that's something good, he got all flustered and knocked over the sugar dispenser. Then told me I had no faith and I was too guarded."

"He sounds like a real bugger, that Heidegger," said the pretty blonde in the pink dress who'd been quiet up until then.

"What did *you* say?" asked the man with the white goatee.

"I told him anyone who opens a café in this part of town has to have a hell of a lot of faith and that if he was to learn anything about philosophy he'd have to spend more time around real people."

"Bravo," said the goateed man. The group smiled and applauded. Frank watched from a distance. He nervously folded and shred cocktail napkins, while scanning the room for help.

"Vince," Frank said, reaching out as the director

approached. “Is he here? Is that psychiatrist here yet? He’s really got to speak to Shelly.”

The director looked puzzled for a moment, then smiled. “I thought you already knew which one he was.”

He turned in Shelly’s direction. The party was gathering more closely around her. She gesticulated wildly, relaying yet another story.

“That’s him over there,” the director said. “The one in the green blazer. The old guy with the goatee.”

The group applauded once again. The old man affectionately touched Shelly’s arm, a prurient gaze flowing from his eyes. Frank felt dizzy, his skin damp and cold; his stomach all prickly as if he’d swallowed a sea urchin. He leaned toward a bookcase, bracing himself as he saw the impossible, Shelly rising upward, her lithe figure floating above the crowd, her silk scarves fanning out like wings, and everyone below gazing up, transfixed into believing.

Event Horizon

Mani wiped his penis on a bathroom towel. Then hurried back beneath the blankets. Wanda's face was pointed toward the ceiling, eyes tranquilly shut. A faint smile poked at the corners of her lips. He rested sideways, an elbow on the pillow and a palm against his warm, happy cheek. He stared at her silently before whispering, "I love you."

"What?" she said.

"I love you."

She turned her head and opened her eyes. "You have to be kidding."

"No. For real."

"You're still drunk."

"I'm completely sober and serious."

Wanda stopped smiling. "Whoa."

"When I saw you this evening at the reception I just got this weird, overwhelming feeling."

Wanda rose from beneath the blankets. Mani looked up, not at her face, but at her breasts. She pulled the blanket to her shoulders. He tugged playfully at it. She pulled back, clutching it more tightly to her chest.

"Listen, buddy, you don't even know me."

"I feel as though I've known you all my life."

"That's creepy. You probably don't even know my name."

"Wendy."

"See! You don't know my name."

"Oh, come on."

"You come on."

"Give me a hint."

"It's Jennifer."

"No, it's not."

Mani sat up to meet her eyes. "When I first saw you, I watched how you took a glass of champagne from the waiter's tray. You looked him right in the eye, like this, and smiled. You were the only person I saw do that. Everyone else just sort of treats waitstaff as non-people. You know? And I thought, Man, this girl is for real. And later when Mr. Brompton made some sort of joke about how many whores does it take to screw in a candle you laughed so hard you spat on his lapel. That was awesome."

"Stop it."

"I think I fell in love with you that moment."

"You're weirding me out. I don't even remember you at the reception. The first time I saw you was in the hallway afterwards."

"Yes! And do you remember what you said?"

"'Do you have a cigarette?'"

"No, you said, 'That bow tie is so hawt.' Like that."

"I was fuckin' drunk."

"A vintage Liberty Dickie bow tie, like Churchill wore. Most girls don't even have an eye for that sort of thing."

"A what?"

"Do you like good Indian food? Look, this is crazy, but I want you to come to my parent's tomorrow for lunch. Do you have a change of clothes in your room? Doesn't matter. I'll take you shopping in the morning. Anywhere you want to go."

"Your parents?"

"They'll love you. And my mother's butter chicken is awesome. Just don't take them too seriously. They like to embarrass me. I never did the stuff they say about the neighbor's turtle pond. I don't know where they get that stuff."

"Look, in no way am I going to your parents."

Wanda slipped out from beneath the blankets. She searched the floor for her dress.

Mani ran to the bureau and pulled the dress out from behind the flat-screen TV.

"I was just looking for that."

"Now hold on a second."

"Look, you're a nice guy. It's been fun. But it's time for me to go back to my room and get some sleep."

"Hear me out first. Because this is important. I'm feeling something I never felt before. Not with anyone. It was like I had this big epiphany earlier. You were down on your knees tugging at my belt buckle and time just sort of froze. Really. I felt like I could live that moment forever."

"Give me the dress."

"I'll give you the dress, but I think we should talk first."

"Give me the dress or I'm going to scream."

He smiled. He liked her playful side.

She squeezed her hands into small fists. "I'm fuckin' serious. Give me the dress."

Mani abruptly transformed. His shoulders rose. Nostrils flared. Veins bulged. Teeth clenched. Eyeballs popped. Knees bent as though about to pounce.

"No!" he yelled.

Wanda recoiled. A shiver ran down her spine and she began to tremble.

Immediately Mani drew back. Shoulders curled. Eyes returned to their dark hollows. A smile pressed against his thick dry lips.

He spoke quietly, almost a whisper. "I got all vulnerable with you and shit. Just laid my feelings bare. The least you can do is talk to me. Tell me what's wrong."

It took a moment before she could speak. She studied her bare feet. The pink nail polish. The white band where she had lost a toe ring.

"Okay. We can talk. But let me put on some clothes. Maybe we can go find some place still open. Have a few drinks and talk."

Mani studied the floral chintz fabric wrapped around his fists. This could be a trick, he thought. Soon as we reached the lobby she might run away.

He went back to the bed and lifted the phone from the night table. "I'll order us room service. Some champagne. Some snacks. You hungry?"

Wanda studied his hands, the yellowy knuckles with their their dark maze of creases. His hands were out of proportion to the rest of his body. Enormous hands. Hands he hadn't yet grown into.

"Ya. Sure. Whatever."

Just keep him talking, she thought. Wait it out. When someone from room service comes I'll get the hell out of here.

He spoke about his sister who wore a veil in public because of a botched nose job. A babysitter who made him eat vomit. A brother addicted to ketamine. A dwarf rabbit named Whitey. A bout of pneumonia that turned his skin blue. A visit to Switzerland to tour the Hadron Collider. A squirrel he once shot with a BB gun. His tears of remorse. The first time he saw a vagina. A science fiction screenplay he was working on about an insatiable toroidal vortex with a sort of consciousness.

"Do you believe in fate?" he asked. "I do. I think

this is fate. Right here."

Wanda brushed her palms nervously across the bed covering. Where was room service? It seemed they'd already waited an hour for a bottle of champagne and two club sandwiches. Then it occurred to her he might have faked the call.

"I've always felt like an outsider. You know that feeling? Like you're a foreigner wherever you go, even in your own family. But with you it's different. It's like at this moment – right now – I feel at home in the world."

Wanda bit her lip, then spoke. "I have to be honest with you. I feel like a real shit. I should have told you earlier."

"What is it?"

"I have a boyfriend back in Sacramento."

"Well, you can't really love this guy if you're here with me. Right?"

She was winging it, trying to get from point A to point B. But the tale wasn't too hard to imagine.

"No, I really do love him. We're practically engaged. We've been together six years. The problem is I – well, look – I drink way too much. It gets a bit out of control. Sometimes I don't even know what I'm doing. Then I end up hurting some nice guy like you. What I really need to do is lay off alcohol. Get sober."

"We'll drink a champagne toast to your future sobriety."

"Please, can we just cancel the champagne? I'm not really hungry either."

"They're probably on the way up."

"It's taking forever. Maybe they forgot about us."

"I'll check."

Mani dialed the phone and spoke to someone on the other end. "I'm not sure. Like thirty minutes ago. Room 6-1-7… Oh, they didn't? Well, don't worry. I was just calling to cancel the order anyway."

He set the phone down and reached for the dress. It was no longer beside him on the bed. Wendy?!

He grabbed his pants and shirt, hopping into them as he dashed out the door. The hallway was empty except for a discarded pack of Double Happiness cigarettes and some crumpled tissue. He turned the corner heading toward the elevators.

No call buttons were pressed. No cars moving away from the sixth floor. He ran toward the EMERGENCY EXIT sign. The stairwell was empty and silent.

At the opposite end of the hall, double doors led to the Horizon's west wing. With bare toes digging into the purple carpeting, he sprinted and shouldered his way through the swinging doors. They burst onto another long corridor. But no trace of Wendy in sight.

There was, however, another young woman. Slumped outside a doorway. She wore a pink crinoline dress, rumpled beneath her like a florescent nest. Her long skinny legs extended into the middle of the hall. One foot in pink high-heels. The other pale and bare.

Mani approached.

"Did you see –"

"Hi," she said. And hiccuped.

"Is everything alright?"

"Can't find my door key."

"I see you lost a shoe too."

"You didn't happen to see one did you?"

There was something familiar about this girl. Not the confectionery perfume. Nor the dolphin ankle tattoo. Nor the way her bottom lip glimmered like a piece of raw salmon. Something sort of cosmological, like the feeling he got when looking through his Celestron up at the night sky, seeing once unobservable bodies emerge fully and spectacularly from nowhere.

As this newfound nebula came to a focus, he felt a trembling in his body, nerve endings catching fire, the pull of gravity attenuating his limbs.

I am a fool, Mani thought. I don't even know my own heart. I've made terrible judgments.

The universe accelerated its expansion. Dark energy rushed in to fill the void. This, he saw, was the true encounter, the one everything led up to. He could not resist its draw. Nor the promise it held of something great, life transforming, just beyond the periphery of this event.

He took the girl's hand, helping her to her feet. Instantly, all matter squeezed in beside him and around him and inside him. Everything contracting to one single point of origin.

The Reagan Years

When Ronald Reagan was governor of California, he had a torrid affair with my mother. He had been married to Nancy for three years at the time he met Mae, my mother. Nancy was a difficult person, my mother said. So was my mother, but in a different way. Nancy was cold-hearted and brutally honest. My mother got along well with almost everyone, because she was solicitous and earnestly insincere. She called it "being politically savvy," and saw it as a necessary burden. She thought Nancy made too many enemies and was not a good wife for Ronald. Perhaps Ronald started to feel the same way and began spending more and more time with my mother while planning his reelection campaign. This, anyway, is what my mother told me on her 58th birthday.

She had met Ronald Reagan on a golf course. The weather turned cloudy, then dark, like the reverse negative of a blue sky. There was a contained stillness and the sense something was about to burst, a beastly storm struggling free from its dark chains. She was playing with two women she'd known for many years, both members of the country club. He was playing with – she couldn't remember.

She says the details leading up to the storm were fuzzy, but she remembered it started to rain, and they all ran toward the same shelter. Only she had fallen behind. Before she quite reached the grove of pines surrounding the shelter, a bolt of lightning crashed close by, so close the ground buckled beneath her and she went sailing into the air.

She passed out. And when she came to, there was Ronald Reagan, former movie idol, and *then governor* of California. That large, kind-faced man with the small eyes and warm smile. He touched her forehead with one hand and held her wrist with another. You would have thought he was a doctor, so certain how to handle the situation.

He raised her up and put his light blue cardigan over her shoulders. She still has that sweater. At least she thought she did. He never asked for it back, so she kept it as a memento and stored it away somewhere. But I've never come across it. And when she died last year I went looking for that sweater but never found *any* cardigans.

My mother was widowed at the time she met Ronald Reagan. Her husband, my father, had been fifteen years older than her and a World War II hero. Killed twenty-two Japanese, single-handed. He was the last surviving member of his platoon. He killed most of the Japanese with booby traps he devised from machine gun parts, bamboo, Wrigley's chewing gum and Lucky Strike filters. He survived the Japanese only to be run over by a drunk ophthalmologist from Cleveland, two years after marrying my mother and six months before I was born.

He came from an incredibly wealthy Missouri family. They owned water. Or something as essential, utilitarian and ubiquitous as that. They sounded to me as if they ran the entire state, that nothing could get done without their approval or their assistance.

They could threaten to leave Missouri and take everything with them, the crops, the buildings, the roads, the rail lines, the sun and the rain. And so people kowtowed to them. Mother had "issues" with her in-laws, but they took her in after my father's death, because of the grandchild, me.

"How come I don't remember them?" I asked.

"You slept a lot as a child, David," she said. "You were very sick. I'm not surprised you don't remember them."

Then there had been a complete and final falling out between my mother and her in-laws. They hired lawyers and planned to bring her to court in an attempt to seize custody over me. They declared her an unfit parent and had false witnesses who would testify that she was a heavy drinker, that she neglected the child, that she was a whore, that she prostituted herself for money and gifts. None of it was true. But when you have money and power, Mother said, you can make nearly anything appear true. In the middle of the night, she packed me up with a few other belongings and we left Missouri, heading west with the changing weather.

In Malibu, she rented a small house on the water. That's where my first memories begin. I remember the beach. The white sand and the dark gray waves. I remember Mother's hands on my belly, pulling me through the cold water, raising me above the waves as they leapt toward the sand. I remember Mother's fingers slipping from my wet skin. And then it was just me, baby boy, caught in the current, being pulled down into the dark angry water and out to sea.

No, that's not a real memory. I couldn't be. It must have been one of those recurring dreams I kept having. It's hard to know for sure.

But I do remember Malibu. We had a maid there,

Justine, a Polish girl who used to fawn over me and carry me in her arms and tease me with her breasts.

"Nah-uh. Those not for you, Svee-pee. Okay, you touch. But jus' a *vittle*."

Justine had family in Chicago. But I think she, like my mother, was running away from family and so had ended up on the West Coast, like so many other runaways, misfits and loose nuts.

I must have been between the ages of seven and nine when Mother started having her affair with Governor Reagan. By then we had moved out of the Malibu house and into a house mother bought in Beverly Hills.

Where the money came from was always a mystery to me. I don't remember Mother ever having any real job. She had *activities* – civic duties, charitable functions, political fund-raisers. She had stocks and investments, too. She was on the board of directors for a major retail chain, though I can't remember which one. And there were always wealthy men with great, cream colored convertibles and burgundy interiors pulling up to the front walk of our house and revving their engines. White dinner jackets and slicked back hairstyles. Floral bouquets.

Roses came to our door almost daily, cradled in the arm of the blue uniformed FTD man, with cards like "Your Wild Tiger – Andrew," "Thinking of you – Stuart" "Darling, these flowers say it best. Yours, Michael." At least that's how I remember it.

Mother says, "Oh there were a few very persistent bachelors on the make, but it wasn't so easy being a working single mother back then. Not one bit."

She rarely, if ever, mentioned Governor Reagan's name, though she worked on two election campaigns for him. It wasn't until he served his second year as US president that Mother began to hint at the affair, sighing as she'd watch his congenial, ax-wielding Camp David figure on the television screen, and say something like, "And to think I knew him all those years ago."

Or, to him, through the TV screen, "Ron, I hope you're finally happy."

It was that old, world-weary version of my mother in her early fifties that began to confide in people about the affair with Ronald Reagan – only after she made certain they would not go blabbing to the media and cause a stink.

"After all, it's just my word. And if reporters come calling with questions I'll simply deny everything."

The year of my eighth birthday, Mother went to Italy for two weeks. There was a scene about it, because she had forgotten my birthday was approaching. Justine reminded her and said she couldn't possibly go. Mother became – well, I remember her becoming very angry with Justine.

"It's not my fault!" she yelled. "I have pressures, you know. So many people I have to keep happy. Of course I know his birthday's coming up. But I didn't think about it when I made the reservation. I can't keep everything in my head at once."

Then later, "Don't try to *guilt* me, Miss. *I'm* the boy's mother, not you. I've made a lot of sacrifices for that child already."

Then later, "Oh, I couldn't enjoy myself in Italy now. There's no point in going. I'll just cancel everything. I don't care. It was my only chance for a real vacation, but I don't care. Screw it."

Then later, after a number of phone calls, "I changed my flight. There's one leaving the evening of the 20th, so we can spend the entire day celebrating David's birthday before I go. See how good I am at working things out so everyone is happy?"

Mother called from Italy to say she was extending her stay another week. She said, "I miss you. Do you miss, Mommy? Be good to Justine while I'm gone. I'll be back real soon."

When Mother came back, she was with a man. A tall, broad shouldered man with wavy dark hair. He looked like a movie star. Thinking back now, I remember he looked just like Governor Reagan. He carried her bags from the trunk of a white Cadillac convertible. He grinned at me, got down on one knee and said, "My, what a handsome young man."

In mother's final year, she was ill with emphysema and cancer. She'd been a heavy smoker all her life and I think it robbed her of her beauty. Her skin turned the color of an old tobacco leaf and became dry and creased. She could not walk anywhere very far without stopping to "take a breather," lighting up a thin, French cigarette. At one time she smoked them from a black holder so her fingers would not smell of tobacco.

In the late sixties, she lost the holder and let her long, red-nailed fingers pinch the ends of her cigarettes as she inhaled them down to the filter. They steadied her nerves, she said.

In the seventies, when I repeatedly encouraged her to quit, she would say, "Quit?! What are you trying to do, kill me?"

She needed nicotine like she needed money. It was something she couldn't live without, something that comprised the very fundamental structure of her being.

"I can tell you all this *now*," she said. She had just had chemo a few days before. Her dark skin seemed clumsily pasted over her skull. She had lost most of her hair and kept her head wrapped in a paisley scarf, as if replacing her dark brown curls with colorful psychedelic orbs. The bright scarf looked ludicrous on this dying woman, but she thought it gave her dignity and a bit of *panache*. On good days she would even apply some lipstick. This was one of her good days and those creviced magenta lips were telling me about Ronald Reagan.

"For three years we'd been seeing each other. It was, I think, not very serious for either of us at first. He had Nancy – *the bitch*. He was dependent on her and I don't think he ever seriously thought of leaving. And I – well, I had you, David. And you were the center of my life and I don't think Ron was much of a family man, really. I mean look how his children turned out – that spiteful Patricia and, oh god, that queer son, Ron. I don't think he would have been a good father to you. He certainly wasn't a good father to any of them."

Outside her hospital window, overlooking Paloma Boulevard, it began to rain. It was the first rain we'd had in six weeks. Car horns blared along the main road, as if people were cheering it on. I wanted to open the window and touch it. But this was a climate-controlled building and the windows were sealed with no hinges or levers.

"David, pull that blanket up for me, would you?"

She began again with her story about her and Ronald Reagan.

"We would both work late at the office and then he would take me to dinner. Sometimes we had weekends together. He suspected Nancy was having affairs of her own, so that made it easy for him to schedule time apart. Usually, he would wait until Nancy said something about needing to go to New York for the weekend to do some shopping or needing to spend a few days alone by the water working on a book she was trying to write. Ha! That woman couldn't write a shopping list without copying one from someone else. Ron thought she was brilliant though. I think Ron liked how she bullied him – a little, anyway.

"When Nancy said she was going to be away, Ron would call and we'd arrange to meet somewhere. We spent many wonderful weekends together like that, until we realized we were both falling in love. Falling in love complicated things. When you start falling in love, you start thinking about the future and where the other person fits into your future or how your future will need to change to keep the other person in it.

"Ron and I were miserable. We were in love but we were miserable, because love – our love – was impossible. Nancy was a powerful woman, one you could not cross, one Ron feared and respected. If he turned away from her, divorced her and married me, she could – she would – ruin him. And I think he knew already he was going to run for President. It was Nancy who put the idea in his head and Nancy who was going to hold him to it. He half wanted that. That's not what I would have wanted. Me, the first lady of the United States?! There's something so gauche in living life that publicly."

Mother didn't look at me while she spoke. She stared straight at the ceiling, but it wasn't the ceiling she saw. She was looking at the past. She was looking at herself at age thirty-five, still pretty, in love, a young, handsome son, a good prosperous life in southern California. And yet she wasn't happy and saw no way toward happiness. She smiled a little, the corners of her lips raised. Was she laughing at how foolish she was? Was she mocking the self-importance she had felt?

"I fell into a real funk, David. Oh, it was awful. I was drinking a lot. I was being a terrible mother. I cried myself to sleep at night, because I was so alone. I was in love with someone I couldn't hold on to. One evening I couldn't stand it any more. I got into the car and drove. I just kept driving and driving. I headed north along the coast. It got very dark and the road became empty.

"I stopped at one of those look out points and sat in the car staring out at the ocean. David, it's so big. All that ocean and no other side in sight. It makes you think about God. Something too big to really understand, but you know He's there. And I said, 'Lord, I want you to stop toying with me. What do you want I should do? Don't make me keep waiting, 'cause life is too short. Tell me now. Or end my life here and now.' I was going to stay there all night waiting for an answer if need be. I got out of the car and found an old hiking path. I decided I'd sit by the water and listen for my answer. When I got down to the water, I saw an old boat someone had pulled ashore.

"It was a crazy thing to do, but you have to realize the state I was in. I pushed that boat into the water and got inside. I said, 'Lord, I'm going to push you to make a decision. Either you take me out to sea and drown me, or you carry me to where I can start my life over and do everything just right.'

"I really was ready to die. I'd had enough. The tide took me out, way out beneath the stars. I could no longer see the beach or the headlights of cars along the coast. It was just ocean and stars. I wasn't afraid, though. I was trusting. Ron always said, 'Trust in faith alone, because no person's ever faithful enough to trust.'

"I started to shake from the cold. I noticed then

my dress was all wet. I thought that had been from pushing the boat into the water, but then I noticed a lot of water in the boat. There was a leak somewhere. And I thought, Well, Lord, I guess you're through with me. I guess I've taken up enough of your time.

"I was half ready to let myself drown. The water came up around my ankles and I knew soon enough it would just pull the boat right out from under me. It rose up my stockings and I could see the ocean rising along the sides of the boat. Was I going to die? Was I really ready to die?

"And then I thought about you, David. I was not a good mother to you, but I could have been. I had wanted to do something to make you proud of me instead of just staying home and being a typical mother. Well, if I were to die like that I would have failed in making you proud and I would have failed in being a good parent. I couldn't bear that. I thought, I am not going to die. I refuse to die until I have another chance at being a better mother."

There were tears in Mother's eyes. They slid down her cheeks, caught themselves in wrinkles, then at the corners of her lips. Her mouth suddenly rose into a smile. She laughed a bit. Then coughed. Then coughed harder and spit into some tissues.

"David, David… It's sometimes like this world is a big damn lie the Lord made up to keep us going. But He's not doing it to be mean. No. Maybe he knows we wouldn't understand the real truth or recognize it if we saw it."

She began coughing violently again. It took several minutes before she told me how she had jumped over the side of the boat, determined to swim ashore, and found the water no deeper than a few feet. She walked her way to shore, shivering with cold and laughing to herself.

Mother did not make it to see the next Millennium. Ronald Reagan did, though. His Alzheimer's was so advanced by then, he had no idea what year it was. Nor could he even recognize his own children. He had turned into a big dumb child, rarely leaving home and incessantly raking leaves from the swimming pool that Secret Service agents kept covertly replacing.

Mother died penniless. Her funeral, like her medical expenses, had fallen upon me, her only living relative. I paid for everything gladly. It was not a huge burden. I lived in Seattle at the time, where, in less than four years, I had gone from earning a living selling ecstasy at raves to becoming an Internet entrepreneur. I had two successful IPO's under my belt, owned stock in numerous software companies and websites, and – on paper at least – I was worth over a million dollars. Just prior to mother's death, I was a consultant for a firm that offered several of the nation's top businesses immunization against the Y2K bug.

Rain poured endlessly the day of the funeral, which partially explains the low turn out. But I also knew from my recent visits that mother had burned a lot of bridges in her life and was no longer on speaking terms with many of her old pals. She was, I came to see, much more like the fierce, combative Nancy Reagan than the savvy, cool-headed politico she pretended to be.

I had been looking forward to seeing Justine, who I hadn't spoken to in nearly twenty years. She moved north, past Santa Barbara, with the neighbor's gardener, the year I entered high school. When she called the the day before the funeral to explain an emergency had come up and she would not be able to attend, I sort of panicked. That night, I slept horribly. I kept having dreams in which waves swept over me, grabbing me with the undertow, trying to pull me away from shore. And the shore was this giant, loose wall of sand I kept trying to climb, never quite getting to the top before another wave came pulling me back down.

I had stupidly left Seattle with none of the Valium I usually take for flights. Nor any Xanax or Inderal. None of my contacts in LA were around or able to help. All I had were a few old E's that had been left in my overnight bag from my trip to Burning Man the year before. The morning of the funeral, I took all three E's, thinking it was the only way to get through the day.

When I think now about that day, I feel embarrassed. I can usually keep my cool while on E, no matter how squishy I feel inside. But I pretty much lost it that day in the cemetery, with the rain streaming down like wisps of silver tinsel from the sky. There were a hundred and thirty-seven shades of green beneath my feet that sparkled and flowed like streams of emeralds. I remember thinking something about the tombstones, how they were not cold granite and marble monoliths, but really more like flesh. And if you squeezed them they responded to your touch and sort of squeezed back in a very subtle, molecular way.

There were only a half-dozen people who attended the burial. I knew none of them. But for that afternoon they were family. They were very kind to me. I don't remember anyone being so kind as those six people. Two of the women were very old, in their late 80's, I suppose. They were like gnarled coastal trees, sturdy and deep rooted from years of living among rocks. They lived next door to Mother during the two years she house-sat in Glendale. They offered to feed me, take care of me, introduce me to their granddaughters. I told them yes to everything.

I left the black Lincoln I had rented at the cemetery and drove home in the back of their limousine, seated between the fleshy, fragranced warmth of these two stately women. At their home, they fed me strawberries and fresh cream.

"Your mother was very fond of strawberries, wasn't she?" said Theresa.

"Yes, I believe she was."

"She was such a handsome woman," said Vivian.

"Yes."

"You're father must have been quite handsome too," said Theresa.

"Yes... Well, I don't know really. I never knew my father."

Ah, the love that radiated from those watery blue eyes of those venerable ladies. Vivian gently poured more cream from the white porcelain decanter onto my bowl of strawberries. Theresa held back tears.

"It's so sad," said Theresa, "Were there any gentlemen in your mother's life you looked up to?"

I could not help myself. I started telling them about the blue cardigan. "It had white buttons of inlaid pearl. It was blue like the sky over Malibu in April..."

They drew their chairs closer to better discern what I was saying. The words poured from me. I could not stop them. I wasn't even completely sure how much of what I was telling them about Ronald Reagan was truth or speculation, because what I was really thinking to myself at that moment was how beautiful life could be.

There were real opportunities for me now. In a few more months, I might have enough money to purchase the ivy and brick house at the end of Vivian and Theresa's street, move my life to Glendale, start a family with the most beautiful granddaughter. This was America. Everything was possible. Everything. If you believed it to be. Morning would come again.

The Great Simanoa

One morning my father woke with a slight limp. He looked tasseled and ruddy-faced, as if he'd spent the entire night on the deck of a ship.

"It was different this time, Ken," he told me, steadying himself with an arm clutched to my right shoulder. "This time I saw the old Simanoa herself."

The Simanoa was the great sea lizard he'd been chasing in his sleep for years. Each night he returned to his unending dream quest, following traces of the Simanoa's carnage as he navigated his steamer through narrow straights and high seas.

To understand these dreams you must first know my father spent many years as the captain of a Merchant Marine ship making runs from New York all the way to the Pacific Coast of Asia. It was a hard job, equal parts back-breaking labor and mind numbing indolence. Not nearly as romantic as how talk of seafaring ways is often made to seem.

"There were great hardships and privations," my father used to say. He spoke of times when provisions ran short and he, as captain, fed the crew on "nothing but dreams" until they made the nearest port.

He had been a great man, well respected – an iconoclast who could not abide by the rigors of wartime regulation, collusion and constraints. He crossed over the line one too many times, though.

When caught flying the fictitious flag of the Federal Republic of Aphasia while in restricted waters, his command was taken away. He was given an office job in Brooklyn near the docks where he posted timetables, administered payroll, registered ships, documented cargo, notarized inspections and looked the other way when necessary.

That's when the dreams first began.

But before the dreams, before the demise of Dad's sailing career, he had actually seen the legendary Simanoa. It was off the coast of North Lombok. The great beast lurched up beside his ship, nearly toppling it with its wake. Then, quicker than any ship he'd ever seen, the Simanoa slipped far out to sea.

That was his one and only sighting of the mighty creature. I can find no one to confirm or deny the event, since his crews were always a nameless, transient lot – uneducated, unreliable and, as Dad would say, unfit for human conversation.

Even Dad, himself, was too easily ready to dismiss the incident as just one ten-minute event in a long life. It was the dreams that mattered to him. And no one could soundly dispute Dad actually saw a Great Simanoa in his dreams.

I was on my way to buy groceries when Dad cornered me with the story of his recent dream, how the Great Simanoa came into view on the horizon, its horned head protruding out of the water, tail whipping a prismatic arc of salt water high into the air. He would have sailed closer if the wind hadn't picked up so suddenly, slamming a fruit crate against his shin and filling the sails with air, dragging him back toward shore.

He savored the sighting all day, going over details with his morning coffee, trying to predict the Simanoa's direction and state of health, planning his strategy should he come upon her in his next night's sleep. Now retired, he could devote his time entirely to such thoughts.

The next morning, after having slept in, I entered the kitchen and found my father holding a raw steak to his right eye. His other hand was busy shoveling forkfuls of scrambled eggs into his mouth. Several brown egg shells lay cracked in the sink along with grease-soaked paper towels from the bacon he'd been frying.

"Morning, Ken," Dad said, his mouth full, yellow yolk and red ketchup caught in his grey whiskers. "She came again last night."

"What? Who?" I yawned. "Who came?"

"The Great Simanoa! Saw her clear as day. She tried to sink my ship with them venomous fangs, but I fought her off but good. Shot a harpoon straight down the ol' gal's throat. Course in all that jostlin' and runnin' about I got myself one helluva shiner."

He lowered the steak to reveal the swollen wound surrounding his eye. It was quite a bruise – deep purple and maroon like an evening sun – and I wondered what Dad had smacked his head against during the night to cause such a swell.

"Sit down. I'll make you some breakfast."

He spryly rose from his seat.

I sat, but could not take my eye off his face – that eye, the purple bruise, the steak juice running down his cheek. Somehow the swelling, the dark coloring and the raw meat clutched in his hand made Dad seem so much younger, like the young man he must have been at one time.

www.ingramcontent.com/pod-product-compliance
Ingram Content Group UK Ltd.
Pitfield, Milton Keynes, MK11 3LW, UK
UKHW020415250726
13967UKWH00007B/2646

9 780957 121317